Advance Praise

"In *What the Living Remember*, Nancy Gerber gives us a
coming-of-age story of a German Jewish boy who turns
thirteen in 1933, the year Adolf Hitler assumes full control
of the German government. Karl Walter faces typical
adolescent "crises": first puppy love; trying to figure out who
he is; loneliness; defining his masculinity. But all these are
textured by the increasing aggression against Jews (boycotts
of Jewish businesses; assaults by Hitler Youth; the Nuremberg
Laws) and the ambivalence of highly assimilated, middle class
German Jews which prevents many from recognizing what is
unfolding before their very eyes. This is an important story
that brings the reader into the psychological world of these
Jews as they grapple with the "social death" they experience
in the pre-war years. It is also a form of Kaddish for the
many who found themselves ensnared in the Nazi death trap,
unable to escape, and who ultimately perished."

> — Ann L. Saltzman, Professor Emerita
> of Psychology, Director Emerita,
> Center for Holocaust/Genocide Study,
> Drew University

What the Living Remember

What the Living Remember

A Novella

Nancy Gerber

Apprentice
House Press
Loyola University Maryland

First Edition

Casebound ISBN: 978-1-62720-272-5
Paperback ISBN: 978-1-62720-273-2
Ebook ISBN: 978-1-62720-274-9

Printed in the United States of America

Design by Alessia Hughes
Editorial Development by Lauren Battista
Promotion by Dominika Ortonowski

Back cover image is a postcard sent to author's father September 11, 1938.

Apprentice House Press
Loyola University Maryland

Apprentice House Press
Loyola University Maryland
4501 N. Charles Street
Baltimore, MD 21210
410.617.5265
www.ApprenticeHouse.com • info@ApprenticeHouse.com

The life of the dead is placed in the memory of the living.

—*Cicero*

Acknowledgements

I would like to express my grateful appreciation to the devoted friends whose careful reading and supportive comments helped guide this manuscript to completion: Ellen Sherman, Fran Bartkowski, Lisa Sturm, Marilyn Papayanis.

To Christine Redman-Waldeyer of Passaic County Community College and editor of *Adanna Literary Journal*, for welcoming me to her classes and publishing my poems about the Holocaust and its aftermath.

To my colleagues at the Academy of Clinical and Applied Psychoanalysis, whose dedication continues to inspire. To Dr. Charles Pumilia, for listening.

To my friends. You know who you are.

To Emily Blumenfeld and Patricia McKernon Runkle of the First Fridays Writing Group, for encouraging me.

To the students at Apprentice House Press and Director Kevin Atticks, for supporting this project and giving it a beautiful home.

To my family: my husband, Bob; my sons and daughters-in-law, Josh and Lesley, Adam and Rebecca; my new granddaughter, Lila; my brother and sister-in-law, Larry and Judy, my nieces Jessy and Emmy and my extended family. You are my hope and ballast.

Preface

Nancy Gerber's *What the Living Remember* tells the story of an adolescent boy in a city resembling Berlin facing the "end of the world." Karl, who turns 14 in the course of this novella, is living in 1930s Germany. He is tested and tormented by bullies at school who are learning to despise him. His mother suffers, sensing the danger growing for Jews, even those like this family who consider themselves more Germans than Jews. His father is a doctor whose Christian patients cut their ties to him due to the race laws enacted after Hitler becomes Chancellor, Führer.

The end of the world as Karl knows it opens on a scene of Karl seeing the red, white and black banners outside the windows of his family's home, "blood-red with a white-hot center…and a black cross on its side with four angled legs." Gerber leads readers to inhabit the daily and the dreadful, and how it tears at and begins to scar this family, their friendships, their work and emotional lives. *What the Living Remember* narrates coming of age at a time of palpable fear, making scapegoats of those deemed different, and therefore, not fit to live among those making the new laws of this country where citizens and neighbors are rendered contaminated strangers.

For Karl the end of the world is also marked by finding and losing his first love on a visit to family in the country. The end of the world is sounded because his father thinks Karl's drawing and painting is unmanly. The end of the world comes in overhearing his parents argue about his father's affair with a woman at his office. The end of the world looms when his best friend's parents are among those who read the signs—and they are increasingly everywhere—and move their family to Amsterdam well before Kristallnacht.

The end of the world becomes yet more real for Karl in the move to New York, to a growing immigrant community of German Jews exiled, banished, fleeing, taking refuge in a new language, new country, with new names and a new self he has yet to become as this novella opens onto his future. Gerber's telling is moving and masterful, offering insights grasped by this writer in our present who deciphers the sense of a past she has never lived.

FRANCES BARTKOWSKI

Rutgers University-Newark
Author, An Afterlife

Author's Note

What the Living Remember is inspired by my father's experience as an adolescent who came of age in pre-war Nazi Germany. Born in Frankfurt in 1922, he fled Germany with his father and sister in late October 1938, a few short weeks before the smashing of synagogues and Jewish-owned businesses in the national government-sponsored pogrom known as Kristallnacht. My father rarely spoke of his past, and I know few details of his early life. The characters in this novella are products of my imagination and my desire to understand what it might be like to grow up as a Jewish child during the Nazi era.

In order to better understand what was happening to Jews in Germany in the years 1933 to 1936, the period in which the novella is set, I consulted a number of books. Those most helpful to my research were Peter Fritzsche, *Life and Death in the Third Reich* (Harvard University Press, 2008), Doris L. Bergen, *War & Genocide: A Concise History of the Holocaust* (Rowman & Littlefield, 2003), and David M. Crowe, *The Holocaust: Roots, History, and Aftermath* (Westview Press, 2008). The United States Holocaust Memorial Museum provides a useful timeline of events on their website.

—N.G.

It's a frigid January morning and red flags are whipping from storefronts and public buildings in the city square. It's very early and *Bergenplatz* is empty and quiet. In an hour or so it will be filled with men and women hurrying to work.

I stand in front of the living room window and stare at the plaza blanketed in scarlet banners. Emblazoned with a white sphere in the center and a black cross on its side with four angled legs, the flags circle the plaza like a regiment. I recognize the symbol of the Nazi swastika, but the banners are something new.

I say to Trudi, "What's happening? Why are there so many flags?"

"Hitler is Chancellor," she says. "He is the new head of state."

"What does that mean?" I ask. People have been talking for months about Hitler. His blinding rise to leadership. His extremism.

Trudi doesn't answer me. Maybe she doesn't know.

I stay at the window for a long time, watching the flags slap back and forth. It's very cold; the windowpanes are nearly frozen. When I hold my palm to the glass and pull it away, there's a print where my hand had been.

"Come away from there, Karl Walter," Trudi says. "It's time to get ready for school."

Trudi turns toward the kitchen but my legs are weighted to the parquet floor. The flags are menacing in the morning stillness, their centers like white-hot coals.

I wonder what Mutti will say when she sees them.

*

Later at Gymnasium, Franz starts kicking me underneath my desk. "You're finished, Zimmer," he hisses, leaning his sharp face across the aisle toward me. His light brown eyes burn with an amber glow, like a tiger's. "My *vater* says all the Jews are done for now that Hitler is in charge." His voice cracks the air like a whip.

"I don't know what you're talking about," I say, queasiness rising in my throat.

Franz is one of the nastiest boys in school. He teases me about my thick curly hair and glasses, tells me I'm too short and don't know how to kick a soccer ball properly. I've told Trudi about his taunts and she says he's a bully, stay away. But she doesn't have to go to school and sit next to him. It's impossible to avoid him. Like an open sore he's always there.

"*Sei Ruhig*! Silence, you two!" says the teacher, and Franz turns away from me and faces the blackboard.

*

Hitler says there's a bright future for Germany except the Jews and their polluted blood are standing in the way.

I heard Papa and Mutti talking one night after dinner. They don't know I hide in the hallway outside the dining room and listen. Mutti told Papa she is very worried, Hitler's attitude toward the Jews is so distressing and ugly. Papa said her concerns are ridiculous nonsense. He reminded her he'd served his country honorably as a decorated army medic. Hitler would never turn against his own people, and besides, we are more German than Jewish. We're not religious; we haven't been to synagogue in years. In fact, we're barely Jewish at all!

There's nothing to worry about; Mutti should stop making herself sick. Hitler is a pompous windbag and meanwhile Papa has a medical practice and a family to take care of.

*

When I come home from school I ask Trudi about Mutti. I want to tell my mother what Franz had said. Are the Jews really done for and what does that mean?

"Your mutti is lying down with a headache," Trudi says. "You can tell her tonight at the evening meal."

"Something happened at school today," I say. "Franz was talking about . . ."

"I can't talk to you now, I have to finish cooking dinner. Don't listen to Franz, I've already told you." Trudi wipes her palms against her apron and disappears into the kitchen.

I go back to my post at the living room window, flanked on either side by heavy woolen drapes. The crimson flags surrounding the plaza continue their salute to the sullen sky.

Mutti doesn't come out of her bedroom for dinner that night and I don't feel like eating. Trudi's shoes tap back and forth in the kitchen. I sit alone at the massive mahogany dining table and push the veal cutlets around my plate. Then I go to my room and watch the shadows from the yellow lamp on my desk march across the walls.

*

I don't remember when Mutti started having headaches. I asked Papa one day if she was very ill and if that's why she is always lying down. Papa said no, these episodes were migraine attacks, nothing serious. "Your Mutti has a lot on her mind," he said. "She is often tired."

"What is she so worried about? Is it Aunt Clara?" Mutti's sister has not been well, with troubling symptoms of lethargy and listlessness.

"I have work to do," said Papa. "Besides, children should not ask so many questions."

Papa is a physician. Among his patients are local businessmen and lawyers and their families. His patients are Jews and non-Jews alike. Mutti says Papa is successful because people trust him. He's very intelligent and well trained. His medal for service as a medical officer in the Great War is framed and decorates the wall behind his desk in the consulting room where he meets with patients.

Papa was born in a small village and always thought of himself as a country bumpkin until he finished his medical studies and came to this city, where word-of-mouth about his diagnostic skills helped expand his practice so much that he has been forced to turn people away.

I walk the few short blocks from our apartment to the building where Peter Steinmetz lives. Peter is in a class behind me at school and Mutti knows his mother from childhood, when Frau Steinmetz used to come for visits. Mutti's father and Frau Steinmetz's father were business partners; together they owned a successful lumber mill that was sold when they passed away, within a few years of each other.

Peter is a good friend. He is quiet like me and we both enjoy playing chess. The Steinmetz apartment, so different from ours, is a bright, welcoming place. Frau Steinmetz collects art. Large abstract paintings with swirling blues and yellows brighten her living room walls. The apartment is painted white, like an art gallery. The afternoon sun streams in through tall windows, filling the place with light. Our apartment is dark and paneled, with somber rugs and thick drapes that block out the sunshine.

When I am with Peter I don't want to go home. Lately Mutti is always in her bedroom whereas Frau Steinmetz sails in and out, carrying parcels from her shopping excursions. When it's time for the afternoon snack she cuts the linzertorte herself and serves it to the two of us, asking about my family and what Peter and I are doing.

Today Frau Steinmetz asks about school, how did the week go? I wanted to tell her what Franz had said about the Jews being done for but I was too shy. Frau Steinmetz is so glamorous and pretty, with large green eyes and auburn hair curling about her face. I thought she would laugh at me and say I was a silly boy for worrying.

Peter is far more interested in the linzertorte than his mother's questions. In between bites he says he's studying decimals and fractions, which are very boring.

"And you, Karl?" she asks. "Are your studies tedious as well?"

"A little, I mean, not so much." I look down at my plate.

Frau Steinmetz laughs, a silvery sound like a bell. She brushes aside some of her copper curls. "I should hope not!"

Then she pats our heads and leaves us alone to finish our cake. I watch her slender frame glide from the room.

*

Arsonists have set fire to the *Reichstag* Parliament building. Nobody knows why. Hitler says it's a Communist plot and all the Communists will be rounded up and arrested. He has ordered President von Hindenburg to issue a new decree: the government can now overrule all state and local laws.

Mutti says she is frightened that Hitler has so much power. Papa says Mutti should stop worrying about Hitler. We have our own affairs to take care of and meanwhile life goes on.

People have been saying the *Reichstag* building, with its imposing Neoclassical pediment and columns, was so badly damaged by flames it looks like a skeleton about to collapse. Hitler's fury about the fire blazes in the newspaper and on the radio but everyone walks around as though there is nothing to worry about. At home the atmosphere is different, tight and suffocating. At night in my room I practice holding my breath to see what it feels like to be gasping for air.

*

Today I was late for school.

This morning Mutti discovered Trudi listening to the radio in the kitchen. Since the beginning of the year all the news broadcasts are filled with high-minded speeches about the glory of the Reich. "The ideal of freedom must become sacred!" the voice of Hitler blares. "The German *Volk* wish to live in peace with the world!" I think he sounds like a farmer's mule.

"Have you lost your mind?" Mutti screeched when she heard the broadcast. "I don't want to hear those filthy lies in my house!" Mutti has never screamed at Trudi before. Trudi was so shaken she burned the oatmeal.

I was running down the school hallway with my satchel banging against me when I saw it: Franz's leg thrust out straight in front of him. But I had too much momentum to stop: I tripped and went flying, collapsing in a heap on the hard wooden floor. Franz guffawed as I went down. "Zimmer, *schwein!* You dirty Jew!" Some other boys were laughing too but I couldn't see their faces because my eyes were burning. I guess that's what I have become, a dirty Jew.

I waited until they all went into the classroom and then I stood and leaned against the wall, waiting for the stinging in my eyes to stop. It would be worse, so much worse, if they saw me crying.

I did not tell Mutti about Franz. I could see how upset she was about Hitler and I didn't want her to get sicker.

And I didn't tell Trudi either. I didn't want Mutti to hear from Trudi that Franz has been bullying me. She would wonder why I didn't come to her first.

*

Trudi has barely spoken to Mutti since the episode with the radio.

She and Mutti have never had a warm relationship. Papa hired her as our housekeeper more than ten years ago because he knew her family from their village. Trudi's father had recently passed away and her mother was taking in laundry as a washerwoman. Papa learned they were destitute.

Mutti has always tolerated Trudi because she's a hard worker and an excellent cook. But the truth is Mutti has never really liked her. I once heard my mother tell my father that Trudi did not behave properly, that she was respectful to Papa but discourteous to her. Papa said he didn't see why Mutti should be so concerned about Trudi's moods.

Trudi does not understand my mother's headaches and her retreats to the bedroom. I know she prefers the lively Frau Steinmetz; Trudi's eyes always brighten when she hears that silvery voice in the hallway.

Trudi is a few years older than my mother. Tall and broad with light brown hair and small blue eyes, her hands are always reddened from washing and cleaning. She has no children of her own and used to be motherly toward me when I was young, listening to my stories about school and books as we sat together at the kitchen table. But lately she has become distant. Maybe she feels it's not her place to chat with me now that I'm thirteen.

*

The *Reichstag* members have voted in favor of the new edict called the Enabling Law. This law allows Hitler to govern without approval from the Parliament. I returned from school to find Mutti sitting at the dining room table, fingers laced together, eyes cast downward at her lap. Her sweater was pushed up a little, exposing her frail wrists. She looked like a wounded sparrow.

She glanced at me and asked if I'd heard the latest about the new law.

"Hitler has destroyed our democracy," she said. "What's going to become of us?"

I had no answer. Her eyes, dark as walnuts, were enormous in her pale face. I'd been hungry when I came in but now I had no appetite. I sat opposite my distraught mother, waiting for her to ask about my day and searching for the right words to comfort her.

*

Today Mutti invited Frau Steinmetz for afternoon coffee. They're sitting in the dining room, enjoying Trudi's sachertorte. The bittersweet scent of freshly brewed coffee drifts into the hallway, tempting me away from my post. But I want to know what's being said so I let the aroma fill my nostrils, knowing it's important not to miss these adult conversations.

Mutti and Trudi are getting along somewhat better. Trudi apologized to Mutti, repeating she was not a Nazi, she was listening to the radio because she was used to doing so before Hitler. "It will never happen again, Madam, I swear it," she said.

Frau Steinmetz tells Mutti that Peter was home with a cold so she did not bring him. I've taken up my regular position in the hallway just outside the dining room. Mutti says something in a very low voice.

"Of course I'm worried!" Frau Steinmetz says.

"What does Max say?" Mutti asks.

Max is Frau Steinmetz's husband. He's a successful photographer, with a large studio near the center of the city where he photographs many of the same families who consult Papa.

Trudi once told me that Mutti and Frau Steinmetz inherited their money from their fathers' partnership. She said their husbands were very fortunate to be married to women who were so well off, whose large inheritances had helped launch their husbands' careers. "Not everyone has such luck," she said. "Hard work doesn't always bring good fortune."

I spy from my hiding spot and watch Frau Steinmetz gently replace the lid on the sugar bowl.

"Max says we have to pay close attention to what's happening. He was not affected by last week's boycott. But everything is changing so quickly. It's hard to know what to do."

Mutti is tapping something, a fork or a spoon, against her plate. If I were doing that I'd get a scolding.

"It's not just what's happening to the Jews." Mutti lowers her voice because Trudi is working in the kitchen. I'm straining to hear but some of her words are lost.

"Otto stays at the office all the time, often very late . . . I think there might be someone . . ."

"Sofie, I'm sorry!" Frau Steinmetz realizes she is speaking too loudly and lowers her voice. "Have you asked . . ."

"Of course not! I couldn't," Mutti says.

"But you're his wife. You have a right to know."

"Otto wouldn't see it that way. He most certainly would not," Mutti says, her voice thick and swollen. She stops tapping on her plate and breathes a heavy sigh.

A hot wave of anger passes through me as I press my back against the wall. Who is this someone Mutti speaks of? Is my father having a relationship with one of his patients? Why would he do this to my mother?

Perhaps Mutti is mistaken. Perhaps my father goes to a bar after work to unwind and delay his return to our home. Why doesn't my mother just ask him how he spends his evenings?

I return to my room and pull out the threads of the wine-colored rug, trying to unravel the mystery of my parents' marriage.

*

Last Saturday the government sponsored a boycott of Jewish businesses throughout the country. Nazi S.A. Stormtroopers patrolled the *Bergenplatz,* brandishing signs proclaiming, *"Deutsche, Kauft nicht bei Juden!"* Germans, Do Not Buy from Jews! in huge, Gothic letters. Frau Steinmetz said she couldn't shop at Baumgart's that day because the S.A. men were blocking the entrance. Someone had painted an enormous Star of David with the words "The Jews are Our Misfortune!" on one of the store's large plate glass windows.

Papa boasted to Mutti that the boycott did not affect him, that none of his patients have left because he is a Jew.

I don't know if I should believe him.

*

Over breakfast this morning Mutti says, "Otto, the government fired Klemperer as conductor of the Berlin *Staatsoper.* Because he's a Jew. Though I heard he converted. Paula Frank just returned from Berlin and says it's all anyone can talk about."

There is triumph in Mutti's voice, as if this revelation will convince Papa we too are in danger. She sets her cup of coffee in its saucer with an authoritative clink.

Papa waves his spoon above his coffee cup and scoffs that what happens to musicians is of no concern to us.

"Otto, Klemperer is a very esteemed conductor. How can you dismiss such news as though it's of no importance?"

Mutti is a devotee of the Berlin State Opera. Before Hitler was named Chancellor the radio used to broadcast their performances. Mozart, Puccini, Verdi—Mutti would sit enraptured for hours at the enamel table in the kitchen, smiling and beatific, transported by the soaring voices and the music. Once I even caught her waltzing by herself as she listened to Strauss's *Gypsy Baron* overture.

"All the Jews in the orchestra were dismissed," says Mutti. "I hear they're planning to go abroad, maybe the United States."

"Not everyone has the luxury of leaving," Papa says.

*

Now they're burning books all over Germany. Last night, the S.A. and the university students built huge bonfires in Berlin's public square, and into the rising flames they tossed books written by Jews and foreigners. Crowds cheered their approval in the darkness as crimson spears of fire rose and devoured page after page, scorching them to ash. Mutti told me Helen Keller was on the list of immoral writers whose books were thrown into the blaze. A copy of Helen Keller's autobiography sits on the bookshelf in our library at home.

"The era of extreme Jewish intellectualism is now at an end!" Goebbels writes in the newspaper. "The future German man will not just be a man of books, but a man of character. And thus you do well in this midnight hour to commit to the flames the evil spirit of the past!"

Mutti weeps as she reads Goebbels' words aloud from the paper. "What kind of people burn books? I don't recognize this country anymore."

Einstein, Freud, Remarque, Kafka, they are all on the list of degenerate writers whose work degrades the German *Volk*. Many of their books are in our library, which once belonged to Mutti's uncle.

Some people are quoting Heinrich Heine, the 19th century playwright. "Wherever books are burned, human beings are destined to burn too." I don't understand what that means. How can you burn people?

I think about the curling flags, blood-red with a white-hot center. Germany is on fire but no one talks about it, as though book burnings happen every day and we should just get on with our lives.

As though words and ideas don't matter at all.

*

When I was young my mother used to read to me at bedtime from Helen Keller's autobiography. The idea that a two-year-old child like Helen could turn blind and deaf from a high fever was terrifying. But when Helen turned seven, her teacher Annie Sullivan arrived to liberate the young girl from her imprisonment, teaching her language by spelling words into the palm of her hand. The story of Helen's accomplishments, among them the first deaf-blind person to graduate from college, were miraculous and inspiring. When my mother read the section where Helen Keller learned to speak German at the New York School for the Deaf, she shook her head. "Such commitment and dedication!" My mother's high school studies had focused chiefly on music and embroidery. She was awestruck that a little blind and deaf girl born in 1880 could attain so much.

I take Helen Keller's book from the shelf and hide it underneath my bed. If Mutti asks for it I'll tell her I've put it in a safe place for protection.

*

Today is *Muttertag*, Mother's Day.

The government has declared Mother's Day an official holiday for the first time. When Mutti heard about it she said she did not want to celebrate a day associated with our atrocious new government. But we ignored her.

Sundays are Trudi's days off but yesterday morning she baked an apple cake for the celebration. Papa presented Mutti with a brooch made of silver and pearls, and I gave her a card I'd made along with some roses I'd clipped from the rosebushes in our garden.

The three of us sit together at the dining table like a family. I listen while Papa tells Mutti about work, his plans for hiring a new assistant and the conference he will attend. His practice is doing well, he assures her; he's seen no change since last month's boycott and the government's ridiculous regulations. Things are certain to get better, or, at the very least, not get any worse. In particular, war veterans have been given an exemption from a new law that prohibits Jews from working in the civil service. As a veteran he is proud the government recognizes the special status and important contributions veterans like him have made to their nation.

Mutti smiles a little. I'm so relieved to see her smile. Papa says he appreciates the effort she is making to recover her health. Mutti promises Papa she will not talk about book burnings on *Muttertag*.

I can't erase the image of scorched books from my mind. Last night I dreamed about our own library, the dark paneled walls and all the bound volumes rising in waves of smoke. I woke up choking on my own breath.

*

Mutti asks me if I would like to spend my summer holidays in Weissendorf with Aunt Clara. Aunt Clara has expressly asked that I come.

I've been to Weissendorf many times with my parents. Omi, my grandmother, still lives in the house where Mutti and Aunt Clara spent their childhood, and Aunt Clara and Uncle Heinrich live in a smaller house nearby.

Aunt Clara cannot have children of her own, Mutti told me, but we are part of a large family and I have many cousins. Some are boys my age who like to play soccer. There is also a girl named Johanna with wavy brown hair and a wide smile, who isn't one of my relatives. I met Johanna at a party last year but was too shy to talk to her. From time to time a girl with dark hair appears in my dreams and extends her hand, beckoning me to follow.

"I'll take you to the train and Aunt Clara will be waiting for you on the platform when you arrive. Then, the week before school starts, I'll visit for a few days and bring you home with me," my mother says.

At first I am saddened when I hear this news. Maybe Mutti doesn't want me around. But then I think of long days here without Peter, who will be traveling with his parents during the summer, and staying home with Mutti, who has returned to closeting herself inside her bedroom. Since the row about the radio, Trudi has become very quiet and barely speaks to me.

"Yes," I tell Mutti. "I'll go."

I'm also thinking I could bring my art supplies and sneak away into the fields to sketch. But I don't say this to Mutti.

Mutti gently places her palm on my shoulder. "I will miss you very much. But I think it's for the best."

*

The last time I had art materials at home was when I was nine. One day I used my last piece of sketch paper and when I asked Papa for more, he said I was too old for such things. "Drawing is not a suitable activity for a boy," he said. "One day you will need to earn a living and provide for your family and knowing how to draw little pictures will be of no help to you."

Papa finds me irritating. He says I'm more like my mother than I am like him. Why can't you excel at sports, roughhouse with the other boys like I did when I was your age, he asks. I'd like to tell him I'm not a mama's boy as I've overheard him complain to my mother.

A few months ago Frau Steinmetz gave me a drawing pad and a set of pencils. She came to Peter's room holding them in the crook of her arm and said Peter had told her I liked to draw on scraps of paper.

I looked at the pad and pencil case and thanked her but didn't take them.

Frau Steinmetz seemed lost in thought.

"You know," she said, "You can always leave them here. I will put them in a drawer in the library so you can take them out whenever you come to see Peter."

"Thank you," I said. "I'd like that very much."

Before I leave for Weissendorf I will take the art supplies from the Steinmetz apartment and hide them inside my desk.

*

I'm sitting in the train on my way to Aunt Clara's. At the station Mutti recognized a woman from our building who is traveling further than Weissendorf and offered to accompany me.

I've taken a seat next to the window, watching as open fields of wild grasses and cottages with peaked roofs speed by. From time to time the woman asks me if I would like a lemonade from the dining car. I'm very thirsty but I don't like to make trouble so I say no, thank you.

At Weissendorf station I spot Aunt Clara, whom I have not seen for over a year. "Karl!" she exclaims, embracing me. "You've grown so much! I almost didn't recognize you."

I'm not tall for a boy my age but thankfully I have grown a few centimeters in the last year. Papa is short and when Mutti wears heels she is a bit taller. Papa does not like this. "*Der Mann ist der Kopf der Familie*," the man is the head of the family, he mutters on the rare occasions he and Mutti would dress for an evening out.

Aunt Clara looks like Mutti, with short dark hair and dark eyes. Mutti told me my aunt has come to terms with not being able to have a child. "It's a good sign she wants you to stay with her and Heinrich," Mutti said before I left. "It means she is ready to move forward."

"You must be famished!" Clara said. "Let's get you something to eat, then we'll pay a visit to Omi and I'll take you around to your cousins."

*

My first Friday in Weissendorf. As Aunt Clara and I sit down for dinner she tells me it's time to light the Sabbath candles. She does this, she says, every Friday, even when Uncle Heinrich is away on business, as he is now. She has bought a challah at the bakery and there's a silver cup with red wine on the table, which is set with a clean white cloth. She asks me if I know the blessings for the wine and bread, and, when I say no, she says she will teach me. They are not difficult and every young Jewish man should know how to say *Kiddush* and *Motzi*.

When the blessings are over, I tell Aunt Clara this is the first time I have celebrated the Sabbath.

"Doesn't your Mutti light the candles?" she asks.

"No," I say. "Papa doesn't believe in rituals. He says they are old-fashioned superstitions and that Jews should behave like their neighbors."

19

Aunt Clara shakes her head.

"I'm sorry to hear that. Your Mutti used to love the Sabbath candles."

I watch as the gold flames shimmer and white wax drips into the elaborate silver holders. I wonder what would happen if Papa came home from work one evening and found Sabbath candles illuminated on our dining room table.

*

The ceremony that recognizes Jewish manhood, becoming Bar Mitzvah, a Son of the Commandments, passed without much fanfare when I turned thirteen last fall. After several arguments with my father, during which my mother reminded him he had celebrated this rite of passage as a young man in his village, I went to the synagogue and stood next to the rabbi as I recited the blessings for the Torah. The words were unfamiliar and strange but my memory is strong and they weren't difficult to memorize. My parents then took me to lunch. And that was the extent of my Jewish education.

My mother gave up so much, her family, her religious practices, when she left home and married my father. Sometimes I wonder whether he had been different, more tolerant and patient when they first met.

*

Life is more leisurely at my aunt's than at home. Aunt Clara lets me sleep as late as I want. There are buns and tea in the kitchen when I wake up and I help myself to breakfast. Then I go looking for Walter and Friedrich.

Friedrich and Walter, sons of my mother's first cousin Charlotte and her husband Albert, are my favorite cousins. Friedrich is my age, thirteen, and Walter is two years younger. The two never sit still, they are always on the go, and when it rains and we're indoors they play pranks or chase each other from room to room while their mother presses her hands to her head and complains they are incorrigible. When the weather is fine, we play soccer or tag or capture-the-flag. We're always busy. It's very entertaining, since every day my cousins ask me what we should we do as if there are so many wonderful opportunities. Because the two are so lively and friendly I do not go off by myself to sketch. I keep my pad and pencils underneath my bed and draw before I go to sleep, after Aunt Clara has wished me good night.

Yesterday there was a letter from Mutti on thick white paper, written in curving black script. It was the first letter I've ever received.

> *Dearest Karl Walter,*
> *I hope you are enjoying your stay with Aunt Clara. The apartment is very quiet without you. Please write and fill me in on everything you are doing.*
> *Papa is at the office many hours. I have been going for long walks in the park. Sometimes I sit on a bench and listen to the children playing. I remember when you were little and we used to bring bread to feed the ducks. You laughed so hard as they raced across the pond to snap the morsels from your hand.*

Papa sends his love and Trudi says she is thinking of you. She has promised to bake a special cake for your return. Write soon.

Your loving Mutti

*

Walter, Friedrich, and I went to a small lake today, three kilometers from the village. Dark fir trees along the wooded path shielded us from the hot sun. Aunt Clara had packed sandwiches of cold meat, which we stuffed in our mouths as soon as we got to the lake. Then we stripped to our underwear and went swimming. The water was chilly and clear. Afterward, Friedrich and I sat on a warm rock while Walter skipped stones that hopped across the surface and then sank to the bottom.

I decided to ask Friedrich about Johanna, whom I hadn't seen since I arrived.

"Johanna? She's in Lausanne with her parents but she'll be back soon. Next week, I think." Friedrich was watching Walter skip stones and didn't snicker or tease me about my interest in a girl. I decided to ask a more dangerous question.

"And the Nazis . . ." I lowered my voice, even though there was no one around except the three of us. "Has anything . . . happened here?"

Friedrich stood up and gathered a few stones. He walked to the water's edge and started skipping them across the lake. I had to stand to hear him. He was facing away from me and speaking in a lowered voice.

"There were some things, this past spring," he said. "Someone painted a huge Star of David on the butcher's window. There was a letter in the mailbox of the town's lawyer, Herr Levi, which said, "Get out of town, Jewish *Schwein*." Mother and Father were worried. They talked about it when they thought I wasn't listening."

Friedrich turned around. "But nothing happened after that. Father told me to forget it, it was a bad dream."

"Are there Nazis here?" I asked. The village was a place set apart; everyone knew each other and families had been living here for centuries. It was unusual for anyone new to settle in and put down roots.

"No, none that I know of. People think there may have been some Nazi sympathizers passing through."

Friedrich and I were silent for a few minutes. There was a chill on my arms, and I could feel goose bumps rising.

"And what about you, Karl? Did anything happen?"

I could have told him about Franz. I thought about what Franz had said, that the Jews were done for, words that still burned the insides of my mind. But I ground my toes into the sand and said, "Not much, really. There was a boycott of Jewish businesses, but we were not affected. My father says the worst is over."

"Yes," said Friedrich. "Mine says the same thing."

*

That night I wrote a letter:

Dear Mutti,

23

I am having a nice visit. Aunt Clara sends her love. Uncle Heinrich has been traveling for business and will be back next week.

I see Friedrich and Walter every day. We kick around the soccer ball or go exploring. Today we went swimming in the small lake behind Aunt Clara's house. The water was very cold. Aunt Clara has been busy with preparations for Omi's birthday party. I wish you were able to come. It will be a large celebration. Please write again soon. Give my regards to Papa.

Your loving son,
Karl Walter

*

Today is the party for Omi's birthday. It's not exactly a surprise. Aunt Clara says that in a small village it's very difficult to keep secrets. But Omi has no idea there will be so many people; at least fifty guests are expected. *Die Ganze Familie*—all the cousins, great aunts and uncles and also close family friends, including Johanna and her parents who have just returned from Switzerland.

Aunt Clara, Uncle Heinrich, and I are the first to arrive. Omi is seated in a large velvet armchair, her silver hair pulled into a bun at the back of her head. Even though it's her birthday she wears a charcoal gray dress. Since the death of my grandfather years ago she always wears dark colors.

She rises to embrace us. We are carrying just a few dishes, to keep Omi off the scent of what will follow. Omi's maid, Maria, comes out to help, bringing the platters into the kitchen. Clara follows her and Uncle Heinrich and I stay behind.

"So, Karl Walter, how are you enjoying your stay so far? I want to hear everything." Omi sits down and smiles, pats the armrest of her chair. "Come, sit with me." She is jovial and friendly. Sometimes I wonder if Mutti was ever like this. When did she become so sad?

"Well, I'm playing soccer with Friedrich and Walter. Sometimes we go for hikes, and the other day we went swimming in the lake."

"*Das ist sehr gut*, to be outside and active," said Omi. "Young boys need to be busy, in the fresh air. And your Mutti? Have you had any letters?" But just as I'm about to answer, the door opens and two more families enter, Friedrich and Walter with their parents and my cousins Sara and Hermann and their parents. The room suddenly becomes very lively; Sara and Hermann are twins, six years old. They carry gifts for Omi, and as soon as they lay them on her lap they start to giggle and tear off the wrapping paper in spite of their mother's protests. Omi laughs and tells their mother not to worry, they are children, after all.

The door keeps opening and guests continue to arrive, Omi exclaiming over and over how marvelous, what a surprise to see so many people! Someone has draped paper garlands above the mantel of the fireplace and over the entrance to the dining room. Hermann finds a roll of crepe paper and begins wrapping it around Sara, turning her into a mummy. Friedrich urges me to join him outdoors, the room is getting so crowded he can barely move. I'm about to agree when I catch sight of Johanna. She's standing near the front window; she must have come in while I was talking to Friedrich.

I say to Friedrich I'll see him soon and approach Johanna, whose face brightens when she sees me. We haven't seen each other in a year. Her brown eyes widen in greeting.

"Hello, Karl Walter."

"Johanna, I'm so happy to see you. How was your visit to Lausanne?"

"So very nice. We stayed in a beautiful hotel on the lake and went for walks and boat rides nearly every day. What about you? What have you been doing?"

"Friedrich, Walter, and I spend most of our time outdoors. Perhaps now that you're back you'll join us when we go for hikes."

Johanna laughs and twirls a strand of her wavy hair around her finger. "I'm not sure what Mama would say if I told her I wanted to run around with a bunch of boys."

I laugh, too. "Well, maybe I can visit you at home."

Johanna looks down at her patent leather shoes as though a ladybug has just landed there. "Maybe," she says.

"Would you like something to eat?" I ask. "I can get you something from the buffet. There's enough food here to stuff a horse."

"I'll come with you," she says. "Then we can sit together and catch up."

I never did go outside to look for Friedrich. I wonder whether he'll ask me questions about my crush on his

26

schoolmate or if he'll be more interested in planning our activities.

*

I can't stop thinking about Johanna. Walter, Friedrich, and I have been up to our usual games but my mind is not really on them. Part of me is wondering what Johanna is doing. Is she thinking about me?

I asked Friedrich a few more questions about Johanna. Who are her friends? What does she like to do in her free time? He is not very interested in talking about her. He seems to think that girls are another species, aliens who don't play soccer. Johanna is one of the best students in school, he says. She is a serious girl who wishes to study science or medicine. Friedrich says he plans to join his father's business and won't have to study at university, thank heaven.

This morning I told Friedrich I would not go for a hike in the afternoon but would see him tomorrow. "Suit yourself," he said. I couldn't tell if he found my defection annoying or amusing.

Later that day I knock on the door of Johanna's house, which is similar to the others in the village, white stucco with brown shutters and a gabled roof decorated in red tiles. The flowers in the garden bloom in purple and yellow, like a Monet painting.

Johanna answers my knock. I ask her if she'd like to go for some ice cream. She disappears to tell her mother and then we walk to the village square. Her bare arm swings gently next to mine, almost touching, and I want to reach for her hand. But I remember what Aunt Clara said about how there are no secrets here. I don't want people to gossip about us.

We eat our ice cream outside as we sit on a bench under the shade of a linden tree. Johanna tells me about the violin, her favorite instrument, which she practices every day for two hours. She talks about her younger sister, Francine, with whom she argues all the time. I laugh at her description of the two sisters fighting over hair ribbons and whose turn it is to walk the dog.

The day is so warm it's hard to keep the ice cream from melting. But suddenly I feel a pressure mounting in my chest. I want to tell someone about what has been bothering me since January. "There's a boy in my class at school named Franz. Last winter when Hitler became Chancellor he told me the Jews were done for," I blurt out.

There. My words are a knife piercing the summer air.

Johanna looks down at the cobblestones beneath our feet. Suddenly I feel sick, as though I've ruined everything.

"I'm sorry," I say. "I shouldn't have mentioned it."

Johanna looks at me. Her brown eyes are very dark. "I know there are things happening. I hear my mother and father talking when they think Francine and I aren't listening. My mother's brother is a lawyer in Berlin. In September he will have to stop working and give up his practice just because he is a Jew. My parents tell us not to worry but I am worried. What is to be done?"

"I don't know. There hasn't been any bad news in a while. Maybe the worst is over." I want to tell her more, about the book burnings and what Heine had written, that

28

when books are thrown into the fire human beings are next. But I don't want to say such disturbing things, as if saying them will make them come true.

We finish our ice cream and walk back in silence.

*

The days are different now. I still look for Walter and Friedrich every morning. Sometimes I find them, sometimes I don't. If they are around, we kick the soccer ball. I never mention Johanna. Friedrich doesn't either.

I go back to Aunt Clara's house for lunch, then take my sketch pad and pencils into the fields behind the village. I put them in a backpack with a few books in case Aunt Clara asks what I'm doing.

I'm not worried someone will see me. I go way back to the end of the field where the tall grasses meet the forest. It's the quietest place I've ever found. Some days I spend whole afternoons out there, sometimes I return for a brief visit with Johanna.

Today Johanna and I are planning to walk to the lake. I told her I wished we could have more privacy and she suggested we visit the small, secluded body of water. She told her mother she's going with a few school friends. I'm not concerned about Friedrich and Walter because they left this morning for a holiday with their parents. But what if someone else sees us?

When we get to the lake I see there's nothing but rocks for her to sit on. I realize she should sit on my backpack, so I empty it and take out my art materials. She asks me about them, and I open the sketchbook and show her some of my drawings.

"These are beautiful, Karl Walter!" she exclaims.

"You are the first person I've shown them to. Besides my friend Peter."

"But why? They are so good, I should think you'd want to show them to everyone."

"My father doesn't approve of my sketching. It's not appropriate for boys, he says. He thinks I stopped a long time ago. I can't tell my mother because I don't want her to tell him."

Johanna reaches her hand toward me. I'm so surprised that at first I don't do anything, then I realize she wants me to take it. I've never held hands with a girl. We sit without talking, holding hands and looking at the silver ripples in the water. We lean against each other and through the cotton of her blue dress I feel the warmth of her shoulder as it presses against mine.

*

Mutti is arriving today by train. She will stay at Aunt Clara's for a week and then we'll return home in time for school.

Aunt Clara has borrowed Uncle Heinrich's car. We stand on the platform, waiting for Mutti's train.

"I can't believe your visit is almost over," Aunt Clara says to me. "It's been such a pleasure having you with us."

Aunt Clara is the younger sister and in many ways she is like Mutti, with a sometime sadness. But there's also a brightness about her that is missing in Mutti.

Sometimes I think it's Mutti's marriage to Papa that makes her the way she is. Uncle Heinrich is nothing like Papa. He is quiet and easygoing. When Aunt Clara asks him what he would like for dinner, where he would like to go for their next vacation, Uncle Heinrich says, "Whatever you wish, my dear." I've never heard Papa say those words.

Mutti gets off the train with her suitcase and glances up and down the platform. When she sees us she drops her suitcase and comes running. Then she pulls me close and wraps her arms around me.

"Karl Walter, I've missed you so much!"

I'm embarrassed about being hugged like this in public but I'm happy to see her. She lets go of me and embraces her sister.

"Clara! You are looking very well, and you've taken such good care of my boy! He's grown brown from the sun."

Clara laughs.

"Dearest sister, I'm so happy to see you. Let's go home and have some lunch."

*

After lunch I tell Mutti and Aunt Clara I'm going for a walk in the fields. But I don't. Instead I position myself outside the dining room and eavesdrop while they drink their tea.

"So tell me, how are things between you and Otto? I could tell last time I saw you together there was some tension."

Mutti clears her throat. She lowers her voice.

"I think . . . there's someone else. I don't know who it is, maybe one of his patients. This past year he has hardly been home, and when he is, he is curt and distracted."

"Sofie." Aunt Clara's voice is full of concern. "That is so wrong."

"It seems like years since we've shared our feelings or gone out for an evening together. Then the headaches started. And I know Otto blames me for them, he thinks I focus too much on my fear of the Nazis. And I worry about Karl. Otto is so distant and cold with him. He told Karl to stop drawing, that it's a waste of time. Karl is a talented artist, did you know?"

"No, I didn't. I've never seen him drawing."

"I suspect he does it in secret. I don't blame him. He shouldn't give it up just because his father wishes he were an outstanding *futballspieler*."

I always knew. I knew my father was disappointed I was not quick and wily on the soccer field the way he was when he was young. But I hadn't known Mutti believed my art was important, that it mattered to her.

"Sofie." Aunt Clara cleared her throat. "I hesitate to say this because I feel I'm interfering. I'm surprised to hear you no longer light the Friday night candles. I remember how you found the Sabbath so soothing. And Karl Walter knows nothing about religion. I've taught him the blessings for the bread and wine. I hope you aren't upset about that."

Mutti sighed. "This is an ongoing battle with Otto. He declares himself an atheist, says Judaism is a hodge-podge of superstitious nonsense."

"And if you remind him it's important to you?"

"I don't think he cares about me anymore. He makes that pretty clear."

"Sister, I don't know what to say. Perhaps Heinrich could talk to him?"

"It would make no difference. Otto will be perfectly charming, the way he is he is with his patients. Then he'll turn around and do exactly as he pleases."

*

The field behind Aunt Clara's house is dotted with yellow buttercups and dandelions. Aunt Clara spreads an old blanket with a frayed border on the long grass in a grove of trees at the edge of the forest. Uncle Heinrich sets down a large picnic basket and proceeds to open a few bottles of beer. "Karl," he says, extending a cold bottle toward me. I take it even though it makes me groggy.

Aunt Clara hands round the sandwiches, thick slices of bread and meat with pickles. The walk has made me hot and thirsty but it's pleasant in the shade and cooling breeze. Mutti tucks her legs under her long skirt and accepts a beer from my uncle. "I wish Mama's arthritis wasn't bothering her," she says. "She does so love a picnic."

There's a buzzing in the field from the insects that make their home here. I stretch myself out on the blanket and listen to the grownups.

"How was your last trip, Heinrich?" my mother asks. "You travel so much these days. You were in Hamburg, I think?"

"That's right. As far as business went the trip was successful. But there was an incident that greatly disturbed me."

I push myself to sit up.

"I was leaving Kirsch's when I saw one of the Brown Shirts club an elderly Jewish man coming out of the synagogue. The man lay writhing in pain on the sidewalk while bystanders just stood there and watched. As I approached a few men appeared from the synagogue. The old man could barely stand. I don't know where the congregants took him. I've never in my life seen such a thing." My uncle pulls a handkerchief from his shirt pocket and wipes beads of sweat from his forehead.

My mother puts her hand to her throat and starts coughing. I worry she'll choke on her sandwich.

"Sofie, are you quite all right? Heinrich, look what you've done! We're here to enjoy the fine day, not to talk about the Nazis!"

My mother recovers her breath and accepts a cup of water my aunt pours from a thermos.

"What would possess you to tell such a story to my sister? You know how upset she gets!"

"Sofie, I'm so sorry." My uncle wipes his brow again. "I wasn't thinking."

My mother lets out a deep sigh. "I'm constantly worried about what might happen to all of us. Sometimes I can't sleep at night. What you've said does not surprise me."

Aunt Clara turns the conversation to village gossip and I resume my prone position on the blanket. I doze for a while and awaken when I hear the clinking of plates and silverware as my aunt packs up the basket. Our picnic is over.

As we make our way back to the house I walk alongside my uncle. We lag behind my mother and aunt, whose long skirts swish against the grass, their arms draped around each other's waists.

*

This is my last day in Weissendorf. Tomorrow morning Mutti and I take the train home. Johanna and I have arranged to meet after supper behind a cottage that is empty because the neighbors are on holiday.

I tell Mutti and Aunt Clara I'm going for a walk and I watch them exchange knowing smiles. Aunt Clara has heard that I spend time with Johanna from Johanna's mother, who told Aunt Clara she thinks I am a well-behaved, respectful boy. Luckily her mother does not know my thoughts about pressing her daughter close to me as we explore each other with our lips.

*

Johanna is waiting for me in a leafy corner of the yard behind her neighbor's cottage. The sky is streaked with pink and gold as the sun makes its way toward the horizon. She steps toward me.

"We don't have much time," she says. "I told my mother I was just going for a short walk."

I put my arm around her shoulder and pull her toward me. I can feel her heart beating rapidly. We kiss each other. Her lips are warm and soft. I've never kissed a girl before. We hold each other and I can feel tears on her cheek.

She pulls away and we look at each other in the dwindling light. I am trying to memorize the shape of her face because I don't have a photograph.

"Karl, I'm so sad you have to leave. When will we see each other?"

Words catch in my throat and I squeeze her hand.

"I don't know. Maybe I can persuade my mother to let me visit you before next summer. In the meantime I'll write."

"I'll write to you, too. I need to go now. My mother will be worried."

I touch my lips again to her mouth and taste the salt of her tears. She turns away and disappears through the gate.

Slowly I walk back in the gathering darkness. Uncle Heinrich and Aunt Clara are in the salon, reading. Mutti has gone to bed, they say. I wish them good night, go to my room and take out my backpack. I open my drawing pad and quickly sketch Johanna's face, shaded by her dark hair. I have trouble drawing her mouth because suddenly I can't remember how it looked just before I kissed her.

*

The first day of the new school year.

During the summer I'd forgotten about the Nazis. Weissendorf is such a small village, far from any of the busy metropolises. My relatives there rarely spoke of Hitler. But here the signs are everywhere. The Swastika, with those ugly black feet that look like stomping boots. In my classroom there's a Nazi flag.

And there's Franz.

Franz has joined the Hitler Youth. I saw him in the park the other day, marching along with the rest of them. He looked ridiculous in his brown shirt and dark shorts. I wanted to yell out, hey you, where's your herd of goats? But of course I didn't. Like me he has grown taller over the summer but he looks a good deal stronger than I am.

The teacher has not put him next to me, which is a huge relief. He's less interested in bullying me now that he's found the Hitler Youth. Every Saturday they meet in the park to sing the praises of the Reich: *"Die Fahne hoch."* Raise the flag! As if there aren't enough of those sickening flags everywhere.

These boys' enthusiasm and loyalty are revolting. What does Hitler stand for anyway? Arresting Communists, burning books, spreading lies and evil stories about Jews, that we are monsters, that we are responsible for Germany's problems. What is it that makes him so popular? Do people feel safer if you lock up everyone who seems different? Sometimes I don't want to live in this country anymore.

I am more like Mutti than I am like Papa, who wants to pretend life is normal. And while the fervent Hitler Youth sicken my stomach, I'm relieved Franz has a new hobby besides torturing me.

*

Mutti and Papa are arguing at the dinner table. Usually they whisper when they talk about Hitler but today their voices echo so loudly I don't have to strain to hear them.

"It's my money, too, Otto! You forget that!"

"Sofie, it's crazy, the idea of putting money in a bank in Amsterdam. I am absolutely against it. There's no need!"

"I had coffee with Emilie Steinmetz. She went to the Netherlands this summer and opened a bank account. In the Netherlands, Belgium, people are worried about Hitler, what's going to happen. It's only here, in this crazy country, where we stick our heads in the sand."

"It's not necessary," Papa repeats. "No one is taking away our money! I promise you, if things get worse I will reevaluate."

Mutti's voice rises an octave to a new register, so piercing I'm afraid the crystal wine goblets will crack.

"I'm telling you, Otto, the time is now, while things are quiet! We don't know what will happen next! Hitler could make another decree and then it will be too late! If you don't do this, I will, I swear it!" Mutti begins to sob.

At that moment I feel a cold anger for Papa. I want to rush into the room and tell Mutti not to worry, if she wants to go to Amsterdam I will go with her.

Then something happens. Mutti takes a deep breath and her voice becomes quiet and icy. She sounds just like Papa. I have never heard her speak this way.

"Otto, I've been putting money aside from my allowance for quite some time. I have enough to open an account. If I need more I will ask Clara to help me."

I hear Papa clear his throat.

"This is not just about you and me," she says. "We have a son. We must consider what's best for him."

Papa coughs.

"Yes, Sofie, you're right . . . If you wish it, next month I'll go to Amsterdam."

"That is what I wish."

Mutti had won! I could not believe it. In the ongoing battle of my parents' marriage my mother had finally prevailed in the face of my father's strong opposition. I wondered if my father would now start to see me as a strong young man with a bright future, someone other than my mother's sheltered, sensitive son.

*

I've had a letter from Johanna! I've already written her twice but this is her first letter to me. And it contains good news.

Johanna has been selected to participate in a young people's musical concert, to be held in Symphony Hall. She arrives next month on 4 November and will stay with her parents at the Hotel Freiburg. She hopes I will attend the performance and that we will be able to spend some time together.

I hadn't expected to see her until the spring holiday, and even then I wasn't certain I'd be able to visit.

I hope the weeks pass very quickly. I'm going to take my sketchpad from the desk drawer where I've hidden it since I came back from Weissendorf. I'll do some quick drawings of Johanna after I've said goodnight to my parents.

*

I'm riding my bike to Wilhelmina Park to meet Peter Steinmetz and kick the soccer ball around. Afterward we sit on a bench as we pass the ball back and forth along the ground.

Peter says, "My parents and I are moving to Amsterdam."

His words are out of place, shocking, like a sudden thunderclap on a fine autumn day.

"Why?" I say. "Everything has been quiet here for a while. My papa thinks the worst is over."

Peter looks straight ahead, as though the Martians have just landed at the far edge of the park.

"My papa's photography business is failing. His non-Jewish customers have stopped coming to the studio. He thinks he can start over in Amsterdam. My mother wants to leave, too. Her brother, my uncle, has been fired from his teaching position at the university. Most of the Jewish professors have been let go. My uncle hopes to move to the United States. My mother thinks we should leave now, before it's too late."

I don't know what to say. Peter is my only friend.

"When is this happening?"

"Not for a few months. Maybe early this spring. Papa has been taking trips to look for studio space. He plans to contact newspapers, too, to see if they need photographers. That kind of work is more reliable, he says."

"I will be sorry to see you go," I say.

"I'm not happy about it. But my mother is determined to get out of Germany. Once she sets her mind on something there's no stopping her."

In my family my mother is blocked by my father. It was a miracle he'd agreed to go to Amsterdam to open a bank account.

"Perhaps you'll like it there," I say.

Peter gives the soccer ball a good kick. We watch as it hits the trunk of a tree.

"I hope so," he says.

After we leave the park Peter and I say goodbye because his mother asked him to stop at the bakery for a loaf of bread. I decide to take a shorter route through the back alleys, even though Mutti has warned me not to do that, it isn't safe.

I round the corner into an alleyway and there is Franz.

He's not alone. There are more boys with him, all of them wearing the brown shirts and black shorts of the Hitler Youth.

"Zimmer, *halt!*" Franz steps in front of me with his arms spread out and I have no choice but to get off my bike. Two of the bigger boys loom on either side of him. The sunshine and crowds of Wilhelmina Park are very far away.

"Where do you think you're going, *Judenschwein?*" he says.

I say nothing.

"Zimmer, answer when you're spoken to!" When he leans his face closer to mine I see flaming hatred in his eyes and veins pulsing in his neck.

"I'm on my way home," I say.

"The little Jew boy is on his way home to mommy and daddy," Franz mimics in a singsong voice. "Now isn't that nice?"

He punches me in the stomach so hard I double over then someone kicks me in the knees. I drop to the ground on the cobblestones. A boy punts my face and I feel my cheek start to burn and swell. Someone takes my glasses and tosses them, guffawing as I grope along the cobbles. I hear my bike bang like a drum against the unforgiving stones, over and over, while hard-toed shoes kick my shins as I try to roll away.

"I don't think our little Jew boy will be riding his bicycle home to mommy and daddy now," Franz says. "Let's go."

They howl in glee like a pack of jackals as they lope around the corner and disappear. I can barely move but I don't want to lie here in case they return. Slowly I reach for my broken bike and limp back to the apartment.

*

When Mutti sees me she starts to wail.

"Trudi, come quickly! Bring some cold cloths! Hurry, hurry!"

Mutti disappears into the library where I hear her ring up Papa. "Otto, you must come home right away! Those little Nazis nearly killed our son!"

Trudi leads me into the kitchen and sits me down. She presses a cold cloth on my searing cheek and dabs some hydrogen peroxide on the cuts on my forehead.

I feel tears sliding down my face because the brown liquid burns so badly, but I don't care. I've made up my mind I'll never go to school again.

"Roll up your trousers," Trudi says.

My shins are bruised with large purple welts.

"Does it hurt?" she asks.

I nod.

"We'll ask your papa to give you something for the pain. Some people are animals."

Gently she places a cold compress against my repulsive Jewish legs.

*

Papa comes home and gives me aspirin and a glass of schnapps, which makes me groggy. I fall asleep and when I wake the room is dark and the curtains are drawn. I've missed supper but Trudi has left a sandwich and a glass of water on my night table. My head is pounding. I'm thirsty but my lips are swollen and sore. I sit up in bed.

Papa and Mutti are arguing in their bedroom across the hall. Their voices are loud and echo against my walls.

"Otto, what are we waiting for? Next time they could kill him!" My mother's voice is shrill and angry.

"Sofie, you are overreacting. He was badly beaten, yes, but they just wanted to scare him. Also, Karl needs to learn to fight back."

"Otto, Karl is small for his age. He's no match for Franz. There were other boys, too. How is he supposed to defend himself against a gang of bullies?"

"I will look into finding another school but I suspect Franz will lose interest now. He's had it in for our son for a long time."

"That's just a temporary solution, a new school. We should leave Germany, as soon as possible!"

"I'm not leaving, I've told you! This is my home. And Sofie," my father's voice is steely, " if we leave we will not be able to take our money. We will have to start over, from the beginning. Our lives will be different, and difficult. And who will sponsor us? We can't just arrive on America's doorstep without a sponsor. Do you understand what I'm saying?"

I knock on my parents' door and open it. My mother is seated before her mirror in a dressing gown and my father is wearing satin pajamas. The roses on the wallpaper seem to pulse in the yellow light. My parents stare at me as though I've risen from the dead.

"*Liebchen*, how do you feel?" Mutti asks. She gets up from her chair and stands before me.

"My head hurts," I say.

My mother places a cool palm on my forehead.

"Maybe you need something in your stomach," Mutti says. "Trudi made a pureed soup. Come in the kitchen and have a little to eat."

I shake my head. "*Nein, Danke*. I'm not hungry." I shut the door behind me, the image of Mutti's dark, sad eyes etched in my mind.

I get into bed and start to shiver. I pull the blankets up to my chin but the shaking won't stop. So Papa thought I should be strong like him. Be a man, fight back, protect

44

myself. How is he protecting us? He is throwing our family in harm's way by refusing to leave.

I clench my teeth and drift off again. I dream I am punching someone who 's wearing the black shorts of the Hitler Youth and steel wire-rimmed glasses like my father's. When I wake up, I imagine telling my father there are many kinds of men, and a man who betrays his wife has nothing to boast about.

*

I am back in class. Mutti let me stay home for a week so my bruises could heal.

Papa could not find a new school. A decree was issued several months ago that limits the number of Jews allowed in public schools. He made several inquiries but everywhere he was turned down, by private schools as well. Schools do not want to open their doors to Jewish pupils.

I am not in any classes with Franz. Papa was able to rearrange my schedule with the principal, who has told Franz his loyalty to Hitler is greatly appreciated but it's not necessary to go to such lengths to show it. Franz will not be punished.

The principal used to be one of my father's patients. Papa would not answer when I asked him if Herr Schmidt still comes to him for consultations.

*

Tomorrow afternoon Papa will take the train to Amsterdam to open a bank account.

I want to leave the country. If we move to Amsterdam I could see Peter Steinmetz and Mutti would live near her dearest friend. Papa says it would not be easy for him to begin again and build a new practice. But maybe Frau Steinmetz could tell people they should consult this brilliant new doctor who just opened an office nearby.

I don't want to go to school. No one looks me in the eye, as though I'm walking around with an infectious disease everyone is afraid of catching. The teachers don't call on me. The days are endless as I sit in silence. Papa refuses to send me to yeshiva but at least there no one would attack me for being a Jew.

*

Mutti is losing her mind. She has been screaming at Papa so loudly I'm afraid her lungs will explode. She rushes into the bedroom and slams the door, only to come out a few minutes later and start screaming again.

In Papa's vest pocket she found a woman's handkerchief. Did Papa take his paramour to Amsterdam? Was that why he agreed to go? How dare he? How dare he!

Papa tries to reassure her, he says must have taken the wrong handkerchief but he is not convincing. I don't believe him.

"Who is this woman! Why have you brought her into our lives! Why are you doing this!"

Mutti is shrieking, tearing at her dark curls. I'm afraid she's going to yank all her hair out.

"Get out! Otto, I want you to leave!"

Papa leaves. The door bangs shut behind him. Mutti collapses in a chair, shaking with sobs.

I am rooted to the floor. I don't know whether to comfort Mutti or leave her alone.

There is no one. My father has left us alone and my mother is beside herself. I don't know what to do. I have nowhere to go. In my room I am like a castaway or a prisoner. I can't read or concentrate. My mind is filled with a dark heat, as though I've put my hand on one of the burning logs in our fireplace.

This is the end of the world.

*

I don't think Mutti meant for Papa to leave. She wanted him to stop seeing the woman. That night I listen to her talk on the phone with Aunt Clara, her voice a crescendo, rising and collapsing. This woman is the unmarried daughter of one of Papa's patients. Mutti asked Uncle Ludwig, Papa's brother. Yes, apparently Ludwig knew. So everyone knows? What should she do? What is she to do?

*

This is the first day at home without Papa. The house is so quiet. Trudi is off from work and Mutti hasn't come out of her room.

I've gone into the kitchen for a roll and some tea. I sit at the small table and strain to hear but I'm not sure what I'm listening for. The clicking of the lock in the front door. The tread of a man's shoes in the front hall.

If Papa doesn't return and Mutti refuses to come out of her room, I'll go to Weissendorf and live with Aunt Clara. Maybe Friedrich will forgive me for choosing Johanna over him. Or maybe he will find a girl of his own and the four of us will be friends.

That afternoon there's a knock at the door. I rush to get it even though Papa has a key.

It's Peter Steinmetz. Would I like to go to his house for dinner?

"I have to tell Mutti," I said.

"She already knows," Peter said. "She telephoned my mother and asked."

When I leave with Peter I slam the front door in case my mother is listening.

*

My birthday. I have just turned fourteen. Mutti gave me a fountain pen. My father telephoned with a brief greeting that left me wanting to ask him when he would return. Trudi made my favorite dessert, *Schwarzwalder Kirschtorte*, black forest cake, topped with candles. She brought it into the dining room after the evening meal and sang Happy Birthday together with my mother. I pretended to be happy. Waves of dejection and anger rushed through me. I imagined grabbing the porcelain cakeplate from Trudi's hands and smashing it on the floor as my mother gasped in dismay.

*

Papa has returned. He was gone for five days.

Mutti rang him on the telephone last night and pleaded with him to come home. I don't think she felt she could go on by herself.

After dinner I hear Papa apologize to Mutti. He has made a mistake, a terrible mistake. He knows he has hurt Mutti and our family. He asks to be forgiven.

"Is it over, Otto?"

"It is over," my father says.

"You've lied to me all this time. Why should I believe you?"

"Because I've come home." This answer seems to satisfy my mother.

My parents' marriage reminds me of a porcelain plate from my mother's wedding set. A few months ago one of the plates fell to the floor and cracked neatly in two. My mother tried to repair it by gluing the two halves together but the crack is always visible, a fine gray line snaking through a field of glistening white.

*

I am sitting in the concert hall with Papa and Mutti, waiting for Johanna to come on stage. She is listed as the second performer on the program.

When she walks across the platform I can't believe my eyes. Where is the girl from Weissendorf? She looks like a young woman now, taller, slender, intense, and serious. She is wearing a navy dress with pearl buttons, her dark hair pulled back and tied with a blue ribbon. She sits on a small stool in the middle of the stage, tucks her violin under her chin, draws her bow, and begins to play.

She plays Kreisler's *"Liebesleid."* Love's Sorrow.

The melody is melancholy and beautiful. In my mind I see the fir trees and silver lake of last summer. The lilting notes make me think of the time we held hands and kissed behind the cottage. I'm reminded of the smoothness of her skin, her soft lips, her heart pounding against my chest.

I want to sit here forever.

When Johanna finishes playing I glance at Mutti. Even in the shadows I can see that tears are sliding down her cheeks.

After the concert we go backstage to greet Johanna. She's with her parents, who invite us to their hotel for supper.

The six of us gather at a table in the hotel restaurant. A waiter in solemn pressed pants and jacket asks us for our order as we sit beneath a crystal chandelier. The table is set with an elegant cloth, china, shining silver. We are patrons of this establishment, just like the other families gathered at nearby tables. The knot in my stomach eases as I forget that I am a hideous Jew. The restaurant is very crowded; the waiter is preoccupied and does not seem to care about our bloodlines.

I place myself next to Johanna as we take our seats; it's all I can do to keep from putting my hand on her knee. At one point our fingers brush against each other. Color rushes to her face and I almost start laughing. Fortunately our parents are so busy talking about the political situation they pay no attention to us. After congratulating Johanna on her performance the four of them forget we are there.

When it's time to leave I manage to have a few minutes alone with Johanna in the lobby while our parents bid their farewells. I tell her, in a low voice, even though no one is listening, that I've missed her, that I will ask my mother to let me visit during the spring holiday.

Johanna says that's a long time from now and she doesn't know how she will be able to wait. I want so much to touch her hair and kiss her but I can't. Our parents would be upset by any acknowledgement of our affection for each other in their presence. So we part, Johanna's hand gently waving farewell.

That night I have a terrible nightmare. I dream I'm trapped inside a burning house. I look through the cracked windowpanes and in the blackness I see Franz. I can't hear him but I can tell by his face that he's laughing. I try to escape but my legs are shackled to the floor. I struggle and struggle while smoke engulfs me.

I wake up feeling as though I'm choking.

I decide not to talk about this dream. Who will listen to me anyway?

*

Today there is a farewell gathering at the Steinmetz's. They are leaving for Amsterdam at the end of the month, earlier than expected. They will celebrate the new year in their new home.

Mutti and I are both losing our best friends. Frau Steinmetz is the only one to whom Mutti can confide the sorrows of her marriage. Peter Steinmetz is the only one who knows about the war between my parents.

There are things I don't talk about with Peter, such as my love of Johanna. On the other hand, he knows about Papa's defection and the clobbering I got from Franz. Everyone at school knows about that.

Peter has never told anyone about my sketchbook, which has been hidden in my desk all these months.

The goodbye party is small, just a few families and their children. On the glass coffee table in the living room Herr Steinmetz has placed photographs of his new studio and their apartment in the center of town, near Leidseplain Square.

Peter and I go into the library and set up the chessboard.

We play without speaking.

Finally I break the silence and ask him when he starts school.

"After New Year's."

Our hearts aren't in the game. Peter is not really paying attention and makes random choices about which piece to move next. As for me, I'm thinking about what life will be like without my friend.

Peter looks up and says, "Amsterdam isn't really that far. Maybe you'll come visit this spring."

I want to see Johanna during the holiday but I don't say so. Peter doesn't know about my feelings for Johanna.

"Maybe," I say.

After a while we've had enough of pretending to enjoy ourselves and return the black and white carved pieces to the lacquered box that belonged to Peter's grandfather. I wonder when Peter and I will play chess again.

*

Mutti's screams at Papa echo beyond the shuttered doors of the library and seem to shake the very walls of the apartment.

Trudi has found my sketchbook. She has never rifled through my desk before and I don't know what prompted her to do so this morning. She showed the book to Papa, who called me into the library. His face was white. His hands were braced on his desk where the book lay open, revealing a drawing of Johanna. It was a shock to see the pages bare and exposed, as though I were asked to stand in front of my father without wearing any clothes.

"Karl Walter. You have expressly defied me."

I could not look at him. I nodded.

"How long has this been going on?"

"Since last spring."

"And how did you get this drawing pad? Did you buy it?"

"*Nein.* Frau Steinmetz gave it to me."

I glanced up as my father's eye began to twitch. The thought flashed through my mind that Frau Steinmetz should be punished, not me.

"Why would she do that?"

"Peter had told her I used to draw when I was younger."

"Karl, it's very serious to disobey your father. Go to your room until I tell you to come out."

Mutti is shrieking that Trudi is not to be trusted, she should not have gone behind Mutti's back, that anything found in my room is something to be discussed with her, Mutti, because she is responsible for what happens inside the home, she is the one who supervises Trudi. Papa says something in a low voice. Although my door is ajar I can't hear the words but I know he must be speaking with that iciness that enrages my mother. The angrier she gets, the colder his voice becomes. From the library I hear books hit the floor. Mutti must be hurling them from the shelves. Finally she yells, "She did this to punish me, Otto, to cause more conflict. She's a troublemaker! I don't trust her and I haven't for a long time!"

Papa's voice rings out. Trudi comes from his village! He has known her family since he was a child. She is not a Nazi sympathizer just because Mutti caught her listening once, just once, to a Nazi broadcast. Mutti really must get hold of herself, her anxieties are tearing apart our family.

The door opens; Mutti is sobbing in the hallway. "Tearing apart the family? Who are you speaking of, Otto? You're the one who has ripped us apart, not me! It's you, with your unfaithful ways! You've destroyed us!"

Mutti rushes down the hall and slams her bedroom door so hard the family photographs in their antique frames shiver on the wall.

*

That night I have a dream about a small village on the edge of a dark lake surrounded by a deep forest. The village is infested with huge rats that scurry in and out of the houses. Franz appears from the shadows of the towering pines, dressed in his Hitler Youth uniform and wearing a green cap. He calls for all the village children to follow him, and when they emerge from their cottages he herds them down to the sea, where they disappear into the black depths.

I wake up shivering and sweating. I recognize Franz as the Pied Piper who drowns all the children. Is that what is in store for us?

*

Once again Mutti and Papa are not speaking to each other. Their silence is as glacial as a tomb. In the aftermath of the argument about Trudi and the drawing pad, Papa seems to have forgotten about my transgression. He has not returned my sketchbook, nor has he punished me. He has not forbidden me to draw. The pencils remain in their case at the bottom of my desk and I can tear sheets of paper from my school notebook, though the lines on the page interfere with my sketches.

I have no wish to draw. Since the theft of my sketchbook, drawing is no longer my private expression. Now that I know Trudi snoops in my room I have to take extra care to lock up this diary, since exposure of what I've written here, especially about my father, would be far, far, worse. The top drawer has a small brass key, which I now keep with me at all times and will continue to do so.

With Peter's departure I have no friends. The other Jewish kids at my school avoid me. They don't want to be seen with me, afraid Franz and his gang of bullies will come after them.

The long hours of the afternoon tick slowly by with Mutti in her room and Papa in the library. From time to time I go to the living room and take my place at the large window. It's very cold outside and the streets are deserted.

Mutti and Papa have forgotten about me. Since it's Sunday Trudi did not come to work, and no one asks if I'm hungry. At supper I go to the kitchen and open the refrigerator looking for leftovers. I sit alone at the small enamel table and eat from a plate of cold meat.

*

At last the war at home is over. I don't know what happened but my parents started talking to each other. From the hallway I heard Papa scold Trudi for snooping and told her Mutti is in charge of everything to do with the household.

There's an eerie calm for the moment but a battle could erupt at anytime. I am relieved and also uneasy.

*

A letter came in today's mail from Johanna, a familiar pale blue paper. I'd written to her shortly after we'd seen each other after her violin performance and I'd been wondering why it was taking her so long to reply. The envelope rested in my palm for a few minutes before I opened it. I studied her handwriting, my name spelled in large, loopy script. Her note felt light and weightless, as if it might blow away.

> *Dear Karl,*
> *I don't know how to tell you this, but I need to tell you before you plan your spring vacation.*
> *Friedrich and I have been spending time together. Shortly after I returned from the concert I realized I'd begun to care for him. We are in the same class at school and see each other every day.*
> *You will be very upset by this news, I know, and it pains me to hurt you. You are so very kind and have been a dear friend. I will always think of you with the greatest respect and affection.*
>
> *Yours,*
> *Johanna*

Friedrich and Johanna. Friedrich had pretty much ignored me the last few weeks of the summer. But at the concert Johanna had been so attentive. When had this attraction to Friedrich begun? I felt like kicking the door and shouting. I went to my room and pounded my fist against the wall. Then I took a pen from my satchel and gouged my desk until there was a small depression. I took Johanna's letters and shredded them over and over until there was nothing left but a scattering of small blue specks on the carpet.

*

A fellow approached me in the hall at school today as I was packing up my books and getting ready to go home. He asked me if I'd walk with him to the *Bergenplatz*, maybe grab a *Kaffee*. His name was Sven, he said. He is in a grade below me and was a friend of Peter Steinmetz. I wondered why this guy with blond hair and blue eyes would want to talk to me. Maybe to ask if I'd heard from Peter.

As we made our way out of school Sven told me his mother is Swedish and his father is a German Jew. I had heard about mixed marriages but I had never met anyone whose parents were from different religious backgrounds.

Sven said he heard about the beating I took from Franz.

"I'm sorry he gave you such a bad time. I feel like you were a scapegoat."

I didn't know what to say. Since Sven's mother wasn't Jewish I wasn't sure what religion he identified with.

As if he could read my mind he said, "We don't think of ourselves as Jewish. But after what happened to you my mother wants to go back to her family in Sweden. She thinks it's not safe here for children of mixed marriages."

I didn't know why Sven was telling me this. I thought he was lucky to have someplace else to go.

We decided not to go to *Bergenplatz* but instead to walk the path that borders the river. There were mothers wheeling carriages, young children with their governesses, older boys and girls on their way home. The walkway was crowded. We found a bench and stretched our legs, cramped from sitting at a desk for hours.

"Many of us felt really terrible about what happened to you," he said again.

I didn't want to talk about Franz. Mostly I tried to forget that afternoon in the alleyway.

"I think you were brave to come back to school," Sven said.

I was surprised to hear this. "What else would I have done?" I said.

"Some of us thought maybe you'd be tutored at home. Or perhaps move in with a relative or close friend in the countryside. My parents said it took great courage to return to Gymnasium."

I had never thought of myself as courageous. It was very satisfying to hear Sven describe me this way.

"So you are saying I'm seen as someone who did not back down?"

"Yes, many of us admire your strength."

I laughed. "Sven, I'd like you to come home with me and explain this to my father."

Sven smiled. "If you wish."

After that, when Sven and I passed each other in the hallways at school we would nod or say hello.

Several weeks passed and I no longer saw Sven in the halls. I found out he had moved with his family to Stockholm.

*

Mutti and I are on sitting in a train on our way to the Steinmetz family in Amsterdam. After Johanna's letter I no longer wanted to go to Weissendorf for the spring holiday. When Mutti asked me why I lied to her and said Friedrich

59

and I had had an argument last summer and were no longer friends.

I could tell Mutti was disappointed; she had talked about a visit to her mother and Aunt Clara. "Maybe I'll go during the summer," she'd said. "You're a young man now, Karl. You're old enough to stay home without me. If you promise me you'll avoid the alleys and stay away from trouble."

Mutti had looked at me with her dark eyes. I could see the fear behind them.

"You don't have to worry," I'd said. "I have no wish to get kicked around like a football again."

Mutti had sighed. I wondered if Aunt Clara knew about the friendship between Johanna and Friedrich and had said something to her about it.

*

Peter and his parents live in a small apartment on a narrow side street. The living space is not nearly as large and grand as their former residence but they seem relaxed and content. Peter told me he likes his new school; Herr Steinmetz has found work as a photojournalist. Mutti and I are staying in a small hotel a few blocks from their home.

Amsterdam is a beautiful city. Canals wind gracefully under arched stone bridges. Everywhere there are people on bicycles. Men and women sit in cafes sipping coffee and enjoying the parade of pedestrians on sidewalks shaded by trees just beginning to leaf. Red and yellow tulips carpet the fountains in the public squares. There are no hideous posters of Jews looking like monsters with huge noses and feral eyes. There are no laws restricting what Jews can and cannot do. What's happening in Germany seems very far away.

Peter and I spend the next few days cycling around the cobblestone streets. I haven't been on a bike since Franz destroyed mine. Neither of my parents has offered to replace it for me; maybe they are waiting for me to ask for a new one. But at home I don't want to ride anymore.

Peter lends me his mother's bicycle. Herr Steinmetz is a good 12 centimeters taller than I am and I can't reach the pedals on his bike. We tried lowering the seat but I was too unsteady and couldn't control the handlebars. At first I was embarrassed to be riding around on a woman's bike but after a while I forgot to be self-conscious. Once again I felt the freedom of my two legs pushing the bike forward as we cycled in and around Amsterdam's picturesque squares and plazas.

One day Peter and I park our bikes at an outdoor café and stop for ice cream. Peter describes his schoolmates, the new friends he's made. The move was expensive, he says; his father earns much less as a photojournalist than he did as a portrait photographer for the wealthy. There's no money to hire a full-time maid. His mother does the cooking.

We both laugh. Frau Steinmetz's cooking failures are legendary.

I remind him of the time I'd been invited to his apartment for Friday dinner. Herr Steinmetz was working late in his studio and the maid had left early for a family emergency.

Frau Steinmetz told Peter she would make a pot roast; after all, how difficult could it be to roast a few pounds of meat?

All afternoon we heard her muttering inside the kitchen as pots and pans banged around and the oven door slammed shut. Finally, Frau Steinmetz called us to sit down. She brought out a large platter and set it on the table. In front of us was a charred mound of beef the size of a man's fist.

"I burned the pot roast," she said.

"It's ok, Mama," Peter said.

"Thank you, darling, but I don't think it's edible. What do you say to scrambled eggs and sausage instead?"

Peter waved his napkin in the air. "Hurray!"

I ask him if his mother's cooking has improved since the move.

"Not at all. For supper we have cold plates or sandwiches. I miss Greta's sauerbraten and Trudi's cakes."

I wanted to tell him I would gladly trade Trudi's dinners and desserts to live in Amsterdam. Our vacation here is coming to an end and I don't want to go home.

*

On the last afternoon of our visit Herr Steinmetz calls me into his study. I'd known Peter's father all my life but this was the first time I'd ever been alone with him. I wonder if I've done something wrong.

He reaches into the bottom drawer of his desk and hands me a handsome gray box.

"This is for you," he says. "I bought it for Peter but he has no interest in photography. My wife told me you often draw and sketch, and I thought you might enjoy another way of looking at the world."

I hold the box in my hands. I'm not sure what to say. I wasn't expecting a present.

"Go ahead, open it." He laughs. "I spoke to your mutti. She thought it was a wonderful idea."

Slowly I lift the lid and remove a dark, heavy object. It's a camera, a brand new Leica. I study the pebbled leather exterior, the lens like a protruding eye, the shiny silver knobs and buttons. I think it's beautiful.

"Thank you but I don't think I can accept such a generous gift," I say.

"It would give me great pleasure for you to have it," he says. "It looks more complicated than it is. We'll all go for a walk later this afternoon and I'll show you how to be a photographer."

*

Papa came to my room tonight after supper and sat at the edge of my bed. I stood beside my desk and waited for him to speak. Was I going to get a scolding? But instead he straightened the crease in his slacks, took off his glasses and cleaned them with his shirtsleeve, and asked how I was doing.

"Fine," I said.

"*Sehr gut.* I'd like to see the camera Herr Steinmetz gave you. Your mutti told me about it."

63

There was a knot in my chest. I didn't know how my father felt about photography. I imagined he thought it was like drawing, a pastime not to be taken seriously, perhaps another assault on his position as head of the family. And it came from Herr Steinmetz, whose wife had given me something verboten, a drawing pad. I sometimes wondered if Papa despised Frau Steinmetz for going behind his back.

I took the camera from its box in the bottom desk drawer and handed it to him. I watched him as he raised the viewfinder to his eye.

"This is a very fine piece of equipment," he said. "Do you know how to use it?"

The tightness in my chest started to ease. To my great surprise he was interested, not angry.

"A little," I said. "Herr Steinmetz gave me a lesson on our last day in Amsterdam. But I need to learn more."

"I can teach you, if you like. I used to take photographs when I was at university."

"*Ist das Richtig?*"

"When I was at university I bought a camera in a second-hand shop. It wasn't a Leica, I can assure you, I could never have afforded something so expensive. After I finished my studies for the day I'd go for walks and photograph the ancient buildings with their stone parapets. Remember, I came from a small village like Mutti's. There was so much to look at in the city. I wanted a way to hold onto what I saw in my mind's eye."

This was the most my father had said to me in a long, long time. So there were visual images that captivated him,

64

gripped his imagination. Maybe he and I have more in common than we know.

*

I have made a new friend at school. Erich Weiss. He's a prankster, like my cousin Friedrich. A few days ago I saw him take a pencil from the desktop of one of our school-mates, a pal of Franz's. He caught me staring and winked. It wasn't much, just a pencil, but still, it was a risky move, especially if Franz were to hear about it.

He's tall, Erich Weiss, 180 centimeters. He likes to laugh. He asked me if we should meet on Saturday and ride our bikes through the park.

I told him I don't have a bike anymore.

"Oh right." He smacked the side of his head. "I forgot about what happened to you last year. Some soccer, then?"

I said it was a good idea.

*

On Saturday Erich and I meet after lunch in the park. We've arranged to meet in the afternoon because the Hitler Youth conduct their marches and exercises in the morning.

The park is not as crowded as usual. From our desig-nated meeting place under the towering maple I see parents and young children at the edge of the pond, tossing bread at the ducks and geese. Then I feel a tap on my shoulder and I jump before I hear a familiar voice call out, "hallo, Karl Walter!"

I turn around and there is Erich holding his soccer ball.

"Who did you think it was? Franz?"

"I wasn't expecting you to sneak up on me like that."

"Right. Well I won't do it again. Let's go toward that clearing over there and pass the ball."

I prefer to go in the direction of the pond where there are other people but I don't want Erich to think I'm scared.

The day is very warm and after a while we decide to sit on a bench. I'd forgotten to bring money with me, and Erich says he thinks he has some change in his pockets so we can buy sodas. We are inspecting the coins he lays out to see if there's enough for two colas when out of nowhere Franz appears and stands before us, hands on his hips.

"Look at these two Jews counting their money. What a picture they make!"

"Beat it, Franz," says Erich. "You're taking up too much space."

Franz moves closer to the bench and pushes his face down toward Erich's.

"You dare speak me to that way, you revolting *Schwein*? How do you know you won't get a beating just like your little friend did not so long ago?"

Before I know what's happening Erich stands and with both hands pushes Franz in the chest. Erich's the taller one and so quick that Franz is caught off guard. He stumbles backward, catches the edge of his shoe on an exposed root and tumbles to the ground.

Erich remains standing, looking down at him.

Franz gets up, brushes the grass from his pants and faces him.

"You've made a big mistake, Weiss. You know I have many buddies and friends who will not like what you've done here. You'd better watch your back, and that goes for your puny little sidekick, too."

Then he spits at Erich. The spittle lands on Erich's neck. Erich grimaces and draws his sleeve across his neck.

Franz laughs and strides away.

Erich kicks at the grass until he turns up a mound of dirt. "I wish I'd roughed him up a bit. I guess that wouldn't have been such a good idea."

We sit in silence. I wonder what will happen next time a gang of Hitler Youth finds us. Erich is stronger than Franz and Franz knows it. Still, Eric would be no match against three or four of Franz's favorite bullies.

"We have to be really careful," I say. "No more trips to the park."

"*Verdammt!*" Erich says, slamming the bench with his fist. "I don't want these shitheads running my life. Say, let's get out of here and get those colas. I have enough money for two."

But neither of us move. After a while the sun seems to vanish and dark gray clouds begin to march steadily across the sky. A raw rain begins to beat against our shoulders. We decide to call it quits and return to our homes.

*

I haven't seen Erich outside of school since that day with Franz in the park. A few days ago Erich asked me if I wanted to borrow his brother's bike. We can stay on the streets that are crowded and busy, he said. But I gave an excuse, I was busy with my family. I will never again ride a bike in my city.

Erich is not Peter. He doesn't like to stay indoors, he doesn't enjoy chess. I think he's found some new fellows from school for his soccer games. I don't know where they play. I don't go to the park anymore.

And so I'm alone again. Sometimes the loneliness beats so loudly I hear it pounding like two fists on a drum.

*

Mutti has left for Weisssendorf. Aunt Clara telephoned and said Omi was very ill; she'd developed pneumonia, Mutti should come as soon as possible. Mutti put down the receiver and held her hand to her throat. Her face was so drained of color I thought she might collapse on the carpet. I asked if I could accompany her but she said, no, don't I have exams?

"I can do them when I return," I said. "This is an emergency."

"No, Karl, you must stay in school and keep up with your studies. Trudi can help me pack my bags and find me a taxi. Once I get to the train station I will be fine."

She called out to Trudi to stop working in the kitchen, she needed her help right away. Then with a sob she rushed to her bedroom, leaving me in the hallway.

*

Aunt Clara called this morning. Omi passed away last night. She will not be buried during the Sabbath so the funeral will take place on Sunday.

Mutti is in a bad way, Aunt Clara told Papa. Shortly before Mutti arrived Omi had slipped into a netherworld, unable to speak. She did not recognize her oldest daughter nor return any of Mutti's attempts to communicate through touch. Mutti has been sobbing for the past few hours and Aunt Clara is worried.

Guilt coils inside my chest. If I hadn't pressured Mutti to go to Amsterdam during the spring break she would have had one last visit with her mother. I wonder if Mutti will ever forgive me.

Papa says we leave for Weissendorf first thing tomorrow.

*

Omi was buried today in the Jewish cemetery at the edge of the village. Many of the same people who celebrated her birthday less than a year ago were there. I stood in the row closest to the grave along with my mother, father, Aunt Clara, and Uncle Heinrich.

Mutti and Aunt Clara wore black dresses with a small tear at the collar to designate them as mourners. Mutti wept silently throughout the brief service. Uncle Heinrich gave the eulogy, since my aunt and mother were too distraught to speak.

"Berta Rosental was a generous woman, beloved by all who knew her. Her kindness, wit, and compassion will be greatly missed. She was not just the matriarch of her family but a respected elder of the Jewish community," Uncle Heinrich said, dabbing at his eyes with his handkerchief. Behind him, the freshly dug grave yawned like a bleeding mouth. As he spoke my aunt and mother bowed their heads.

When it was time to toss handfuls of dirt onto the coffin as a final farewell, my mother fell forward on her knees as if about to throw her body onto the traditional pine box in which my grandmother rested. My father and Uncle Heinrich each took an arm and supported her as she stood and slowly made her way past the grave.

*

After the ceremony we went back to Aunt Clara's. I filched a small glass of schnapps from the dining room to stop the shaking inside me. Many people approached to offer condolences. Friedrich shook my hand solemnly and said Great Aunt Berta had always been so kind to him, he was very sorry for my loss. I wanted to tell him he should be sorry for stealing Johanna away from me but I nodded and said nothing. From the corner of my eye I could see Johanna near the window twisting the blue sash on her dress. She looked up and our gazes caught for a brief moment. I could feel her hesitation, see the question in her glance. Had I forgiven her? And though I felt it was wrong to refuse her apology at my Omi's *shiva*, I turned away.

Mutti will stay with Clara for the week of mourning but I'm returning home with Papa. Mutti had asked me if I wanted to stay, adding that since I'm not a mourner and not expected to sit *shiva* perhaps I want to get back to my schoolwork? I did not want to return to school but I didn't want to stay in Weissendorf and imagine Friedrich together with Johanna. I told my mother I would take the morning train home with Papa.

*

Mutti has been much worse since she returned from Omi's funeral. Many days she doesn't get dressed and wanders around the apartment in her pale satin robe. Her face is distracted and drained of color. Sometimes she smiles at me as though she doesn't know who I am. When Trudi asks what meals she should prepare for the week, Mutti waves her hand in the air and says anything will do.

I ask Papa what can be done to help her. Papa says if she doesn't improve soon she may have to go to the Burgholzli hospital in Zurich where she can be taken care of. I don't understand why we can't take care of her at home.

"What kind of place is Burgholzli?" I ask my father.

"It's a sanitarium with good rates of success for patients with mental disturbances. There's a whole program of activities and different therapies, much more than we can provide. I've asked my colleagues and they tell me it's a reputable institution, one that is highly suitable for your mutti. Herr Doktor Carl Jung used to work there. You've heard of him, perhaps?"

I had not heard of Herr Doktor Carl Jung but I nodded.

A year ago Hitler proclaimed the Law for the Prevention of Progeny with Hereditary Diseases. This edict enforces sterilization of those afflicted with mental diseases. Mutti and Papa have never spoken of more children, but what if Hitler found out and Mutti was sterilized?

I was in hospital once, when I was six. The halls were very white, I remember, and very cold. I had broken my arm in a bad fall from my bike and had to stay overnight. Mutti and Papa were not allowed to remain with me, and I was placed in a room where strange shapes threatened me from all sides. Sometime during that endless night I heard the door creak open as a nurse entered, her white dress and cap illuminated and ghostly. She stayed a moment or two, then turned away without speaking and left me alone again.

I hate to think of Mutti alone in a darkened room, weeping all night long. Who will comfort her when she cries for help?

*

Mutti has been in bed for the past two weeks. When I enter her room to say goodnight I find her curled on her side facing the wall. I put my hand on her pillow and tell her *Gute Nacht* but she does not speak.

This morning there has been some improvement. To my surprise Mutti emerges from her room and sits down at the dining room table. She asks Trudi to bring her a cup of hot coffee. Her hair is unwashed and disheveled and her expression is not right; there's a hollowness in her eyes that reminds me of an Edvard Munch painting I had once seen at the art museum. Still, I'm happy she has finally risen from her bed.

"What has been happening?" she asks as I sit down for breakfast. "I've lost track of time."

"Everything is as it was," I say. "Do you feel better?"

"A little. I have not been doing a very good job as a mother, have I?"

"You've always been a good mother. I was so worried about you."

"I'm sorry to have caused you so much concern. I think things will be better now."

"I'm glad. Papa and I have been waiting for this."

"Your papa, does he come home at night? I haven't always seen him."

"Yes," I say. "He's been sleeping in the guest room so as not to disturb you." Thankfully I was telling the truth.

"I see. And school? The term has come to an end?"

"In a few days. I'm finishing my last exams."

"I'm wondering if you'd like to go to Amsterdam this summer. I could write to Frau Steinmetz and see whether a visit is possible."

"Yes," I say. "I would enjoy that very much."

My camera is sitting in its gray box at the bottom of my desk. I haven't taken it out since my conversation with Papa. I'm not in the mood to take photographs of my city. The camera is a tool with which to see the world more sharply, to focus on what is worth remembering. I have no wish to record the ugly, shadowy fear that clings to everything here like a curtain of smoke.

*

I never made it to Amsterdam to visit Peter Steinmetz. My train ticket had been purchased but then von Hindenburg died and Hitler declared himself Führer, Leader of the German Empire. The radio announced that later this month a referendum would be held to approve Hitler's control of the government.

The day of von Hindenburg's death Mutti and Papa sat opposite each other in the dining room. Mutti shook her head so violently I thought her neck would collapse. Papa sat in silence, raking his fingers through his thinning hair. Papa's silence upset me even more than Mutti's sobs; this was the first time I had seen him so rattled by the political situation.

"Well, Otto, what do you say now that Hitler is our dictator? What is going to happen to us?"

"Sofie, I need some time to think. It does no good insisting you've been right all along. No one could have predicted this. From what I understand, Hitler has violated the Constitution by changing the laws of succession."

"Oh, Otto, wake up!" Mutti exclaimed. "Who's going to enforce the Constitution? The Nazis?"

"Let's see what happens with the referendum," Papa said. But I could tell he did not believe there would be a change for the better. His voice trembled with the shock of the defeated.

A few weeks later voters went to the polls and said yes to Hitler. He is our Führer. To violate his rule is a crime. And the *Volk* approve.

*

School has become a prison. Nazi flags hang in all the classrooms. Every day we are forced to stand and pledge allegiance to the Führer: "I swear by God this sacred oath: I will render unconditional obedience to Adolf Hitler, leader of the German Reich." I move my lips as though I am speaking but do not utter the words. If one of my school-mates were to recognize my disloyalty I would be expelled.

The teachers speak about poisoned Jewish blood, about how our presence contaminates the Reich. We Jewish kids hang our heads and say nothing.

What's the point of going to school? We are not able to participate. No one expects us to contribute; we are not wanted. When the teacher came around for our essays this morning he passed right by me without stopping to collect the sheets I held out in my hand.

*

Trudi quit today. She chose to tell Mutti while Papa was at work, when she knew Mutti would be home alone.

This happened as I was getting ready for school. She and Mutti were in the kitchen; I could hear them clearly from where I sat in the dining room finishing breakfast.

Trudi said her mother was not well and that she planned to return to her village to live with her. She was giving my mother two weeks notice.

"But Trudi," Mutti said. "You have a sister who lives with your mother. Surely she's looking after her."

"Madam, I am the oldest child. It's my duty to be responsible for her care."

"Perhaps you can wait, at least until I find someone to replace you, which may take more than two weeks. I don't know how we will manage without you."

"I'm sorry Madam but I cannot wait any longer. You've just lost your mother. You know how precious time is."

It was impertinent for Trudi to speak this way and also hurtful, since Mutti complained frequently and loudly that she felt guilty she did not have a chance for a last farewell with Omi before her death. But Trudi and my mother have been very cool with each other for a long time.

I waited for Mutti to reply that while Trudi was working for her, she did not expect to be spoken to in such a tone. But instead there were a few moments of silence followed by the shattering of a cup on the floor.

"After all these years this is how you treat us!" Mutti's voice was sharp, cracked like the cup she'd just broken. "Go now, pack your bags and leave, this moment!"

"Madam, I can ask around, it will be difficult . . ."

"Go, you ungrateful creature, I don't know how I've managed to have you in my home this last year. You hate us because we're Jews! Pack your things and get out!"

It did not take Trudi long to gather her belongings. She'd often stayed with a sister who lived on the outskirts of the city and didn't keep much in her tiny room off the kitchen. She ran through the dining room and called out a quick farewell to me as she flew by. Then the door shut behind her and she was gone.

Trudi had worked for our family for more than 10 years. Now there is no one to do the household chores. Does my mother even know how to cook? How are we going to manage?

*

Later that evening before going to bed I enter Trudi's room off the kitchen. It is small as a nun's cell, with a cot, a narrow wardrobe, and a nightstand with a low lamp. I sit on the edge of the bed and wonder if Trudi had ever liked us and whether we had paid her well. This room was just like other maids' quarters I had seen. Still, Trudi had grown up in the same village as my father. I wondered if she'd resented the differences in their station.

I sit for a few minutes and on an impulse I open the wardrobe. It's empty save for the bottom shelf, where there's a poster like the ones handed round at rallies. I reach for it and stare. Before my eyes is the figure of the Führer wearing full military dress, a fist clenched at his pocket and the other hand at his waist. Below the portrait is a slogan in large bold type, *Ein Volk, ein Reich, ein Führer!* One People, one Empire, one Leader!

My mother was right about Trudi after all.

*

Mutti has not been well since Trudi quit. She sits in her satin wrapper on the sofa in the library and stares at the books on the shelves as though waiting for them to speak. She barely eats or drinks.

Papa has hired the receptionist from his practice to come to our apartment three afternoons a week to prepare supper and do some light cleaning. Mutti will not engage with this woman, Christa. When Christa started working she would ask Mutti if there was anything special she would like to eat, could she make her a hot cup of tea? Mutti either ignored her questions or turned away. Christa has stopped asking.

She's a kind-hearted woman, Christa, patient with Mutti and friendly to me. Still, the air in the apartment is suffocating while Mutti continues her mute stare into the emptiness before her.

*

I came home from school today and dropped my satchel in the hallway as I always do. When I entered the living room I found Mutti pacing back and forth, weeping and pulling at her hair. She wasn't wearing a single stitch of clothing. Her skin was as colorless as a corpse.

I felt my legs sink into the floor. I wanted to run to her side but I couldn't look at my mother without her clothes. I had never seen a woman this way, let alone my own mother.

"Mutti," I called out. "I'm here now. Everything will be all right. I'll be right there."

I hurried to her bedroom and yanked a robe from the armoire. In the living room I stood behind her as I wrapped the pale satin around her and gently guided her emaciated arms through the sleeves.

I led her to the sofa and helped her to lie down.

"Where is everyone?" Where are they?" she kept say-ing. "What's happened to Omi? Why haven't I seen her lately?"

"I'm here now," I repeated.

In the library I picked up the telephone and rang my father's office. Christa answered.

"It's my mother. Something has happened to her. Tell my father he needs to come home right away."

"What's happened?"

"My mother is extremely distraught. She's beside her-self. Tell my father. He'll know what I'm talking about."

*

Mutti, Papa, and I are sitting in a taxi on our way to the hospital. Papa has found a place for Mutti in a small sani-tarium at the edge of our city, a place where Jewish doctors still practice. When I asked him why not the Burgholzli, he said Switzerland was too far, it would be difficult to visit. I wondered if he thought once Mutti left Germany it might be difficult to bring her back.

Mutti is slumped in the backseat, head hanging forward like a little girl's rag doll. I'm sitting in the back with her, the black valise Christa packed squeezed between my legs and the driver's seat.

At the hospital we help Mutti out of the taxi. She lists to the side like a small boat about to capsize. I carry her suitcase and Papa holds her around the shoulders as we step into the cold gray waiting room.

"Stay with your mother while I let them know we've arrived," my father says.

I gently take my mother's arm and help her settle onto one of the small hard chairs that line the room. Her dark eyes are vacant, as though she does not recognize anyone or anything.

My father returns shortly and tells me her room is ready now; we can bring her upstairs. A nurse will meet us there.

*

The room is stark and white with a narrow bed framed in metal and a light curtain that divides the space. Through the thin cotton I see the outlines of another form, a head on the pillow, a body covered by a blanket. I'd imagined Mutti would have privacy but there are no sounds or movement coming from this nameless woman.

A nurse enters shortly after we seat Mutti on the side of the bed. She asks us to leave for a moment so she can help Mutti into her hospital gown, then we can come back and say our goodbyes.

My father and I stand in the hallway, my father clasping and unclasping his hands. I've never seen him this way, uncertain, ill at ease. When the nurse opens the door he strides ahead of me as if he's once again in charge. I watch as he bends over Mutti, who lies on her side facing away from him, and brushes his lips against her cheek. Then he turns to me and tells me to say adieu.

Mutti's arm, frail and translucent, rests atop the coarse hospital blanket. I wish we'd brought her a quilted comforter from home, something soft and familiar. I bend to kiss her cheek. "Mutti," I whisper. "Get well so you can come home soon." My mother's eyelids flutter, the only sign she has heard me. I swallow hard and follow my father out of the room.

*

Each day after school I drop my schoolbooks, make myself a snack of cheese and bread, and wait for the tram that will take me to the hospital to see my mother.

She has not improved since my father and I said our goodbyes a week ago. This afternoon she is propped up on a few pillows, eyes shut. Her dark hair is matted, her skin white as paste. I pull a chair next to her bed and say hello. She does not speak or open her eyes.

"Mutti," I say. "It's Karl Walter. Can you hear me?"

Silence.

"Mutti." My breath is choking inside me. "Please say something or nod your head so I know you hear me."

Mutti flutters her fingers on the blanket.

"Shall I tell you about school? Or would you like me to read from Hellen Keller's autobiography? I brought it with me today."

Mutti does not reply.

I open the leather-bound copy of *The Story of My Life* and read aloud.

> *"It is with a kind of fear that I begin to write the history of my life. I have, as it were, a superstitious*

hesitation in lifting the veil that clings about my childhood . . . ."

I try to modulate my voice, hoping the rhythm is more soothing than the words I recite.

After a few minutes I notice Mutti's hand drifting toward me across the hospital blanket. I look around for the knitted throw I brought from home but don't see it anywhere.

I close the book and stand.

"Mutti," I say. "Aunt Clara is coming tomorrow."

Mutti's fingers hover in an arpeggio. I bend down and touch my lips to her parched cheek, wishing the arpeggio was meant for me.

*

Today as Aunt Clara and I are putting on our coats to go to the hospital, we hear the telephone ring in the library. We look at each other.

"I'll get it," Aunt Clara says, rushing to halt the insistent ringing.

A few minutes later Aunt Clara returns, her face slack as melted wax.

"It was your mother's nurse," she says. "Your mother has developed a serious infection, from the contagion of strep throat they believe, and has been placed in quarantine. They don't want us to visit for now."

Aunt Clara slowly walks into the living room and sits in one of the burgundy armchairs. She leans forward, pressing her palms to her temples, and lets out a long moan that twists itself around the room.

"I'm sorry, Karl Walter, I know you're worried, too."

I enter the living room and sit opposite her in the matching armchair.

"When can we visit? Does my father know?"

"The nurse asked me to call your father. She doesn't know when we can come. They are waiting to see if your mother can fight off the infection. She is very weak right now."

I feel a tightness move from my chest into my throat. I think about how Mutti resisted my father when he first refused to open a bank account in Amsterdam. I have no idea how much strength it takes to battle a raging infection.

My mother hasn't spoken to anyone, including Aunt Clara, since she entered the hospital. She seems to have lost the wish to live.

*

The telephone rang in the middle of the night. I struggled with sleep, thinking my alarm clock had started buzzing by mistake. Then my parents' bedroom door opened and I heard my father's footsteps in the hallway. After some time the door to my room opened and my father leaned against the jamb. A dim light from the hall pierced the darkness but his face was hidden in shadow.

"Karl Walter, are you awake?"

"Yes," I said.

"I have bad news." He entered the room and turned on the switch on my small desk lamp. I pushed myself upright into a sitting position.

"That was the hospital. Your mother has passed away. The cause of death is sepsis." He gave a dry cough and placed his hand briefly on top of my head.

I waited for him to break down in tears or sit at the edge of my bed and reach for me. But he continued to stand next to the mattress and look down at me.

"We cannot have the funeral until Sunday, because of the Sabbath. I believe you have a suit from Omi's funeral, is that right?"

I nod, though I have no idea whether it still fits.

He touched my head again. "I'm sorry, Karl Walter. This is hard on all of us. Your aunt is beside herself."

Then he turned off the lamp and left the room. When the door shut behind him I turned my face into my pillow, soaking the pillowcase with my tears.

*

We are burying my mother today in the Jewish cemetery behind the old synagogue not far from our apartment, beneath the limbs of a giant spreading oak. Before Hitler my parents purchased a plot here, agreeing they would be buried together in the city where they had made a home.

We are a small group: my father and me, Aunt Clara and Uncle Heinrich, my father's brother Uncle Ludwig, one of the nurses from my father's office, and Frau Steinmetz with her husband and Peter. I wasn't expecting to see them,

84

thinking they would never return to Germany. There are also a few men from the synagogue to make up a *minyan*, the group of ten males needed to recite the traditional prayer for the dead, the mourners' *Kaddish*.

Aunt Clara, my father, and I stand in front near the rabbi, the collars of our dark clothes bearing a small tear. When it comes time to say the *Kaddish*, I hear my father's voice chanting in Hebrew, strange and yet also familiar. *Yitgadal v'yit kaddash sh'mai rabbah.* I am old enough to recite this prayer but can't, since I've never been taught the words. A deep anger rises in me, that I cannot mourn my mother in the language of my family's faith.

My father has asked Uncle Heinrich to give the eulogy. My uncle praises my mother's dedication to her family, her gentle spirit, her love of music and flowers. A woman of valor, he calls her, from the Book of Proverbs. I shovel a clump of dirt into the open wound of my mother's grave, remembering how my mother nearly collapsed at her own mother's funeral. My knees buckle a bit as the soil hits the coffin. The shovel burns in my fist and I want to hurl it like a javelin across the expanse of silent headstones. But instead I mutter, "Mutti, I will miss you," as I feel someone take my elbow and lead me away.

At the apartment Christa quietly sets platters on the table while the guests speak in muted voices. I sit on a bench in the living room with an untouched plate of food on my lap. Someone has covered all the mirrors with bed sheets, in keeping with the Jewish custom of mourning.

Peter Steinmetz approaches and places himself next to me. We sit together not speaking; I'm in no mood to talk about chess or life in Amsterdam. After some time he gets up and walks away. Frau Steinmetz takes his place and places her arm around my shoulders. I can smell her perfume, a scent like lilacs. The sweetness reminds of my mother, who used to dab rosewater on her neck. My mother loved roses and sometimes would cut a few from the rosebushes in our garden and place them in a small vase near her bed.

"I'm so sorry, Karl," Frau Steinmetz murmurs. "This is such a terrible thing. I can't imagine how you feel."

"Thank you," I say. "For coming." I can feel Frau Steinmetz's grief mixing with my own and I want to rush out of the room.

"Oh Karl." A sob escapes from Frau Steinmetz's throat. "I loved your mother. I've known her since we were girls." She starts to shake. "I'm so sorry. She was your mother. She loved you so much. I hope you know that."

"Yes, I do."

She touches my shoulder gently and the smell of lilacs spins round me again. I wait for her to return to the other guests, and when she does I go to my room. I lay down on the bed with a gaping emptiness in my chest and think about my mother asleep in a sealed coffin covered by layers of rocks and dirt.

*

My father has begun to talk about leaving Germany. Uncle Ludwig moved to New York a few months ago, aided by one of his close friends who'd fled last year. My uncle has said he will sponsor us, since immigration laws require an American sponsor. Without a sponsor, we would not be allowed to enter America.

We are eating breakfast at the dining room table and drinking coffee. Since Mutti's death Papa has learned to do a few things for himself, including making coffee.

Every now and then he grimaces as he drinks the bitter brew. "*Ach*," he says, "at times like this I miss Trudi's excellent *Kaffee*." He does not mention my mother's name unless I bring it up, which I often do.

"If we leave this place we will never visit Mutti," I say.

"Your mutti wanted us to leave." My father doesn't look at me as he stirs cream into his cup.

"Why now? What's changed?"

He drums his fingers on the table. "Your uncle told me people in New York are very concerned about what's happening here. They don't understand why we remain in this place where we're not wanted, where we've been kicked out of government, universities, newspapers. Ludwig is pressuring me to get out as soon as possible. What are we waiting for, he asks? Even though," my father adds, "things are very quiet at the moment."

Now that my father is considering leaving the country I don't want to go. I think of my mother buried in a corner of the old Jewish cemetery, her granite headstone recently engraved with her name and dates.

Sofie Zimmer, Geb. Rosental.
22 January 1897 – 19 October 1934.
Beloved wife, mother, sister. Forever Remembered.

For eternity my mother will sleep alone. Her family is buried in the place where she grew up, in Weissendorf, not here in this city we are about to leave. When we depart her grave will be forgotten.

And New York, a giant metropolis, larger than any in Europe. I've grown used to the speeches and decrees here, the Hitler Youth, the hideous posters, the sneers and silences from my schoolmates and teachers. I don't speak English beyond the little I've learned at Gymnasium. What if life in this new place is even worse than it is here?

As if my father can read my thoughts he says, "There's a large German-Jewish community in a neighborhood of New York City called Washington Heights. Ludwig tells me he hears German inflections all the time, in shops and on the streets, people from Mannheim, Hamburg, Frankfurt, Berlin. No one is afraid to say they're Jewish. 'Don't worry,' your uncle tells me. 'You and Karl will feel right at home.'"

"It's what your mother would have wanted," my father adds.

An image hovers in the corner of my eye, a pale opalescent face framed by wavy hair and melancholy eyes. And I know my father is right.

*

On the train to Weissendorf I stare out the window at the green fields rushing by and think about my mother, how she never returned to the village of her birth after my grandmother passed away.

When it became clear my father was seriously considering leaving our homeland, I told him I wanted to say good-bye to Aunt Clara and Uncle Heinrich.

Last night my father called me into his bedroom and handed me a black velvet box. Since my mother's death I have avoided this room with its memories of her presence. Her rosewater scent somehow still lingers in the air, though the yellow roses on the wallpaper seem to have withered.

"What's this?" I said.

"I'd like you to give this to your Aunt Clara. I'd like her to have something that belonged to you mother."

I opened the box. It was a necklace, a cluster of wine-colored garnets surrounded by filigree.

"I remember this," I said. "Mutti used to wear it when she went out."

"It was a birthday gift I gave to your mother. Garnets were her birthstone."

I shut the box. "I don't want to give this to Aunt Clara."

My father gazed at me in surprise. "Why not?"

"I remember Mutti wearing this necklace," I repeated. I did not want to tell him someday I would be married and hoped my wife would treasure the necklace and wear it as my mother once had.

My father sighed. "Very well. Choose something else from your mother's jewelry box. Although," he added, "we must be very careful. Our suitcases will undoubtedly be searched at the border. Anything of value will be confiscated."

"I'll wrap it in cloth and hide it in in the toe of my shoe. No one will think to look there."

My father emitted a rare chuckle. "True. I've heard of people being asked to empty their pockets but not their shoes."

Then his expression turned somber. "At least, not yet."

*

I've brought the Leica with me to Weissendorf. Alhough I never took it out of its box to photograph my city, I've decided to document this small place that meant so much to my mother. Yesterday I walked to the lake where Friedrich skipped stones and I sat with Johanna that long-ago summer. I took some nice images of the towering fir trees reflected in the depths of the rippled water.

Later today Aunt Clara and I are to visit Omi's grave. Aunt Clara asked me to accompany her. She will teach me the prayer for the dead, the mourner's *Kaddish*, although as a grandchild I'm not supposed to recite it. "I want you to know this prayer," she said. "Not for Omi but so you can pray at your mother's grave before you leave Germany." Then she began to weep.

"*Ach*, Karl, so many people are leaving. Heinrich and I hope to go soon. I've spoken to your father, who says he will sponsor us when the time comes."

"Who else is leaving?" I wanted to know if my aunt was speaking of Johanna.

"A few families I've known for many years. They are not people you've met. It's more the feeling of disappearance. First Omi, now your mother. I imagine you know just what I'm talking about."

We were sitting in the salon and Aunt Clara was gazing out the window toward the fields, in the direction of the cemetery where Omi was buried. I had no wish to see Omi's grave but I did not want to disappoint my aunt.

I didn't know what to say to Aunt Clara. Her sadness was so heavy I felt it would crush me beneath the weight of my own. We sat in silence for a long while.

Finally I said, "It's very hard to leave behind those you love."

Aunt Clara wiped her eyes with a handkerchief. "Yes, *mein Kind*, it certainly is."

*

My last full day in Weissendorf, and I decide to walk into the village after lunch. I've brought the Leica with me so I can photograph the square with its quaint shops and rustic stone fountain where children throw pennies.

As I approach the square I hear a familiar voice call my name. I turn and there's Johanna, standing beneath a linden tree.

"Karl Walter, won't you come and talk with me a few minutes? I've heard the news you're leaving soon for America."

I walk slowly toward Johanna, my legs moving ahead but my mind a swirl. We have not spoken to each other since her violin concert.

"Please, sit with me for a while," she says, taking a seat on a bench. "Friedrich is away on holiday," she adds, as if it's important that I know.

"I wanted to tell you how very sorry I am for everything. For the way I treated you, and the loss of your mother. You must hate me." She places her hand on the bench near my leg. I move my leg away.

"I could never hate you, Johanna."

"You must be very angry with me."

I say nothing. I want to tell her I will always remember her, the silkiness of her hair on my neck, our kiss behind the cottage.

"It was a long time ago," I say. "So much has happened."

"Yes, that's true. It's all so confusing and hard to believe."

We both stand.

"Won't you at least shake my hand, as a sign of friendship?" she asks. "Who knows when we'll meet again?"

I take her hand and hold her fingers, small yet strong. I want to ask her about the violin but instead I blurt out, "What was it about Friedrich?"

We are standing in the shade of the tree but I see the color rush to her cheeks. She turns her head slightly away.

"Oh Karl, this is so difficult. Friedrich and I have known each other since we were children. Perhaps we were meant to be together."

This does not answer my question but I have no wish to continue talking.

"*Auf Wiedersehen*, then. I wish you good luck," I say.

"And I wish the same for you."

*

In the newspapers and on posters throughout the city the following announcement proclaims that Jews are no longer considered citizens of Germany.

THE LAW FOR THE PROTECTION OF GERMAN BLOOD AND GERMAN HONOUR

Moved by the understanding that purity of German Blood is the essential condition for the continued existence of the German people, and inspired by the inflexible determination to ensure the existence of the German Nation for all time, the Reichstag has unanimously adopted the following Law, which is promulgated herewith:

Article 1.

Marriages between Jews and subjects of the state of German or related blood are forbidden. Marriages nevertheless concluded are invalid, even if concluded abroad to circumvent this law.
Annullment proceedings can be initialed only by the State Prosecutor.

Article 2.

Extramarital intercourse between Jews and subjects of the state of German or related blood is forbidden.

All through the city men and women gather near the posted announcements of the Nuremberg Race Laws, then hurry away. The news travels through us like shock waves. Jews have lost the protection of the government. We are no longer Germans; we are stateless aliens. Our presence is a danger to the Reich. The threat of who we are, impure and unwanted in the eyes of the state, horrifies us.

That night at dinner, my father clears his throat. "It's time to leave. This is no longer our home," he says.

Fear sits right beside me, silent and invisible, pulling at me with long, clammy fingers.

We are leaving next month. My father has booked passage for us on the *Neue Amsterdam*, a ship departing from Rotterdam. We will stop first in Amsterdam to close the bank account my father opened and bid our goodbyes to the Steinmetz family.

*

Our final weekend in the country of my birth. My father and I have gone to say farewell to my mother. It's less than a week from the one year anniversary of her death.

We place ourselves in front of the granite stone that announces the finality of my mother's life, the end of her struggle with melancholia. My father and I stand without speaking. We place small round stones on the headstone as a sign of respect. After a while I can bear our silence no longer and begin to speak.

"Mutti, you are greatly missed. We think of you often and pray that you have found peace." A sob rises in my throat and tears slide down my cheeks. I glance at my father, whose face glistens with small droplets.

We recite the mourner's *Kaddish*, a prayer I have memorized. Jewish law requires I recite these words in my mother's memory. Never again will I be without the knowledge of this benediction.

Later that night I wonder if my father was weeping out of guilt for the way he treated my mother or from the traces of a painful love. As I toss in bed I realize how difficult it is to really know my father. He hides everything, much like the negative of a photograph.

*

Our last night at home. The apartment is empty save for the beds in which we sleep and the small enamel table in the kitchen with two wooden chairs. My father and I have each packed a suitcase and placed them next to each other in the hallway, where they huddle against each other like a pair of frightened twins.

My father hired an appraiser to sell our furniture and china, crystal, silver, the books in my mother's library. I've packed Helen Keller's autobiography at the bottom of my suitcase. Though my father asked me not to take books, they are heavy and, while not valuable in monetary terms, might ruffle the border guards, I've decided to take my chances. The Leica, freed from its handsome box, has been carefully wrapped in layers of shirts and sweaters.

"All our belongings will be sold for a pretty penny," my father told me after the appraiser left. "But what can I do? Herr Bayer was willing to pay me in cash."

"How will you get all that money out of the country?"

"Well," my father said. "It's not as much as you might think. I had to buy our tickets for *the Neue Amsterdam*, and then some funds went to the ticket agent who was expecting something off the top. And then I need some for the Nazi officials when we reach the border. But between what I have left and the account in Amsterdam we'll manage."

That night I climb into bed but can't sleep. Images of Mutti and the heavy granite stone above her grave float through my mind. I toss back and forth, back and forth, then there's a knock on the door.

My father enters and leaves the door slightly ajar. The light from the hallway traces a triangular shape on the floor.

My father is holding something in his hand and places it at the edge of the bed. It's my drawing pad, the one Trudi found in my desk and gave to my father nearly two years ago.

I'm astonished. I'd assumed my father had tossed it in the trash.

"I thought you might want to pack this," he says. "It won't take up much room."

Then he walks away. At the door he stops and half turns toward me.

"I'm sorry, Karl," he says as he shuts the door behind him.

My father has never apologized to me before. His words quiver in the room like the wings of a moth. I will take them with me when we leave.

*

At the *Café Americain* Herr Steinmetz raises his wineglass to toast my father and me. "To your health and prosperity in America!"

"*Prost!*" and the five of us clink goblets.

It's a fine early afternoon in Amsterdam, quite warm for autumn, so we sit outdoors beneath a striped awning as we eat our meal. In the evening we will board a train for the short trip to Rotterdam.

Today marks the anniversary of my mother's death. It's eerie and sad to be saying goodbye to our friends on this, our final day in Europe, the very day my mother passed away a year ago. I wait for someone to say something.

There's an awkward pause and then Frau Steinmetz clears her throat. "I don't want you to think I've forgotten Sofie, your dear mother." Frau Steinmetz looks directly at me. "I know today is her *yahrzeit*. I keep her memory in my prayers and thoughts."

If my father and I were observant we would light a candle and recite the *Kaddish* at my mother's grave. Instead we are sitting in a café toasting with friends.

"Yes," my father says. "The timing is very awkward. I had difficulty arranging passage and this is what was available. My hope is that Karl and I honor Sofie by our decision to go to America. I regret fighting so hard against her wishes."

My father is not one for public displays of emotion but his voice trembles. He seems deeply shaken by our departure from Germany.

Herr Steinmetz bows his head. "Let us remember dearest Sofie, taken from us before her time. May she rest in peace."

"May she rest in peace," we repeat.

The air tightens around as us memory draws us into its circle.

*

We live now in Washington Heights. Our apartment on Fort Washington Avenue is small and very dark. Our living room window opens onto a dingy courtyard paved with broken concrete and my bedroom overlooks an air shaft. Rents are quite expensive here, my father tells me. But my uncle was right; everywhere I go I hear a familiar accent and sometimes even my mother tongue. The German-Jewish community has its own German-language newspaper, *Aufbau*, a name signifying reconstruction. I'd like to freelance there as a photographer even though I'm a teenager, as they say here.

My father has enrolled me in George Washington High School, where many of my classmates are also German Jews. There is a sense of camaraderie among us and the relief of living without fear. Though none of us speak about it, I have the idea I'm not the only one who was beaten and bullied in Germany. We are glad to be in a new country, safe from the Nazis. Still, we have all left loved ones behind. We do not speak of this, as if to do so would bring harm to those who live in the Reich.

My father is mortified that he must work as a nurse until he learns enough English to take the medical boards so he can practice again as a physician. Between night school and hospital work he is exhausted and irritable.

I spend my afternoons at home doing schoolwork or at the apartment of one of my new friends. My schoolmates are eager for my friendship; I've found a way to make them laugh. In Germany no one thought I was funny. Here people my age seek my company, they find me amusing. In this new place I've found my voice. I've been invited to join the amateur soccer league that meets in Fort Tryon Park in the spring.

In a few months Aunt Clara will join us. Last month Uncle Heinrich unexpectedly suffered a heart attack and passed away. Although Aunt Clara is now completely alone, she continues to delay her voyage. My father says he understands; fear of the unknown is disabling. In one of her letters she wrote about moving to Brussels to live with Heinrich's sister. *We are your family,* my father wrote back. *Please come to New York. You can stay with us until we help you find a suitable place. It would mean so very much to Karl Walter.*

*

On November 11, 1938, the following news appears in the *New York Times:*

> *"A wave of terror swept over Germany yesterday, destroying nearly all Jewish businesses, burning most of the synagogues, and landing thousands of Jews in jails and concentration camps. 'If I were a Jew, I'd remain silent,' said Joseph Goebbels, Minister of Propaganda. 'There is only one thing Jews can do—shut up and say nothing further about Germany. German people will not tolerate having their rights*

curtailed or provoked by the parasitic Jewish race.'''

My father and I left Germany just in time. We hear many stories—bank accounts seized, borders closed, property ransacked, men clubbed on the streets and sent to a detention camp called Dachau. I am sickened by the thought of what will happen to Jews still living in the fortress of hatred that is the German Reich.

War has been declared against Germany. People I knew in high school will serve in the army, fighting on behalf of the Nazis. Many of the Jewish kids I know are trapped inside Germany, including my cousins in Weissendorf and Johanna. I try not to think about what will happen. There is nothing I can do to help. I pray to a deity I don't know to please protect them and keep them safe.

*

I receive a postcard in the mail. I don't recognize the image, which is dark and faded, of a park somewhere, with a shadowy figure underneath a large tree. There is no return address but the postmark is Rotterdam.

> *Dear Karl,*
> *I cannot say much, but we are well for the moment, staying with family friends.*
>
> *I think of you often.*
> *Your friend,*
> *The White Knight*

I know right away this message is from Peter Steinmetz. The White Knight was his favorite chess piece.

The Nazis invaded the Netherlands on May 10. It is not safe to be a Jew in Holland. How could Frau Steinmetz have known that Hitler's tentacles would reach so far? I fear for my friend and his family.

*

I spent the war years at Fort Dix, performing menial tasks in the kitchen and mess hall. I was not sent overseas because of my poor eyesight. After the surrender of Japan I resumed my studies in journalism at Baruch College, from which I will graduate next year.

My father has a successful practice as a doctor in Washington Heights where he treats other German-Jewish refugees. He has a lady friend named Hilda, also a German Jew. She and I are cordial with each other but we are not close. My aunt Clara lives in an apartment near my father and works as a secretary. We see each other often. Although she never remarried, she has adopted a slow, gentle bulldog named Butchie, of whom I am very fond even if he is the laziest canine alive.

I'm engaged to a young woman named Margot whose family fled Berlin following Kristallnacht. We met at a dance three years ago. She is petite and slender, with a bob of brown hair and dark blue eyes. She is quite strong and athletic, having excelled as an athlete before being forced to quit when she could no longer attend public school. Her kind smile and warm laugh remind me of Johanna. Margot and I plan to marry after I graduate with a degree from Baruch.

Two months ago I went to City Hall and legally changed my name from Karl to Charles. I am now Charles Walter Zimmer but everyone calls me Charlie. My name was too identifiably German, and now everyone hates anything to do with Germany. I've been trying hard to erase my accent but when I leave Washington Heights people always ask me where I'm from.

As for the Jews . . . no one wants to talk about what happened to the Jews. Those of us who survived lost family, friends, our first language, our homes, our country. But we're living our lives and the others are not.

This is something we cannot speak of. We're ashamed to be alive. We're ashamed to be angry about what we've lost. So we hide our shame and pretend that life is grand, that what happened in the camps never really happened at all.

"Forget the past," we tell each other. "Live in the present." And that's what we try to do. But sometimes, when I'm alone in my room at night, surrounded by darkness, I turn my face to the wall and pray to the dead for forgiveness.

*

On my nightstand I keep a photograph in a silver frame. Pictured there are a young boy and his mother, both wearing the same style of swimsuit, a black tank. The mother, pretty and dark-haired, also wears a silk scarf round her neck. Together they walk along a sandy beach. Behind them stretches a long, low pavilion with an awning and lounge chairs, where families take shelter from the midday heat and sun.

Before them is the future. Only one of them will arrive.

*

And thus Heinrich Heine's words, that after books are burned people come next, were enacted in the crematoria at Auschwitz-Birkenau, Dachau, Mauthausen, Bergen-Belsen.

I write now to remember those who never returned:

Peter Steinmetz and his parents, who perished at Auschwitz. Friedrich, who lost his life at Buchenwald.

Walter survived, the only survivor of his immediate family.

Johanna and her little sister Francine, who met their deaths at Bergen-Belsen.

Erich Weiss, lost somewhere in the graveyard of Europe.

In memory of the dead I recite the mourner's Kaddish.
Yitgadal v'yitkadash sh'mei raba.
B'alma di'vra chirutei,
V'yamlich malchutei. . .
Glorified and sanctified be G-d's great name through-
out the world
Which he has created according to his will.
May He establish His kingdom in your lifetime and
during
Your days...

I recite these words to remember.

In every photograph I take of my new city in my begin-again life, I see the shadows of their faces.

After all, mourning is an act of remembrance.

Epilogue

In 1939, eighty-three percent of Americans were opposed to the admission of refugees from Europe.

By the end of the war, ninety percent of Jewish children in occupied Europe had been murdered.

About the Author

Nancy Gerber received a Ph.D. in English from Rutgers University and completed training as a psychoanalyst at the Academy of Clinical and Applied Psychoanalysis in Livingston, New Jersey. She is the author of five books, including *A Way Out of Nowhere: Stories* and *The Dancing Clock: Reflections on Family, Love, and Loss.* She has also published a chapbook of poems illustrated with family photographs entitled *We Are All Refugees*, which explores the effects of Holocaust-related trauma and exile on her father and family. She maintains a private psychoanalytic practice in New Jersey.

Apprentice
House Press
Loyola University Maryland

Apprentice House is the country's only campus-based, student-staffed book publishing company. Directed by professors and industry professionals, it is a nonprofit activity of the Communication Department at Loyola University Maryland.

Using state-of-the-art technology and an experiential learning model of education, Apprentice House publishes books in untraditional ways. This dual responsibility as publishers and educators creates an unprecedented collaborative environment among faculty and students, while teaching tomorrow's editors, designers, and marketers.

Outside of class, progress on book projects is carried forth by the AH Book Publishing Club, a co-curricular campus organization supported by Loyola University Maryland's Office of Student Activities.

Eclectic and provocative, Apprentice House titles intend to entertain as well as spark dialogue on a variety of topics. Financial contributions to sustain the press's work are welcomed. Contributions are tax deductible to the fullest extent allowed by the IRS.

To learn more about Apprentice House books or to obtain submission guidelines, please visit www.apprenticehouse.com.

Apprentice House
Communication Department
Loyola University Maryland
4501 N. Charles Street
Baltimore, MD 21210
Ph: 410-617-5265
info@apprenticehouse.com • www.apprenticehouse.com

www.ingramcontent.com/pod-product-compliance
Lightning Source LLC
Chambersburg PA
CBHW060333260626
47160CB00007B/2789